# DRIVING CRAZY

Blue Deco Publishing
www.bluedecopublishing.com

Driving Crazy

Cover by Colleen Nye
proofreading staff: Sue Kaminga, Rosalie Sanara Petrouske,
Lori Hudson, Jason Smith, Candy-Ann Little, Jesse Goldberg-Strassler and
Mark Hein
Formatting by Colleen Nye

Published by Blue Deco Publishing
PO BOX 1663 Royal Oak, MI 48068
BlueDecoPublishing@gmail.com

This is a work of fiction. All characters and situations appearing in this
work are fictitious. Any resemblance to real persons, living or dead, or
personal situations is purely coincidental.

# REVIEWS FOR DRIVING CRAZY

"Driving Crazy ... is an unusual, entertaining debut novel by a highly talented writer."

-- Ray Walsh, Lansing State Journal


"Entertaining and witty, Driving Crazy is (an) enjoyable work of fiction."

-- Retro Gamer Magazine


"I picked it up last night and ... stayed up until 2:30 AM to finish it. Once you start it, you can't put it down. At multiple times throughout the book I found myself laughing out loud."

-- Brian Fullmer, AtariAge.com


"A truly enjoyable read that should be made into a movie!"

-- Jay Smith, Jaguar Sector II

To Wendy,
I waited a lifetime to find you,
but you were worth the wait.

**ONE**

The excitement bubbled through me, pumping so powerfully I could no longer remain seated in my computer chair. I leapt to my feet and began dancing around the house yelling, "Woo-hoo! Who da man? I da man!" My poor cat Heidi had no way of understanding my raucous jubilation, so she freaked out and dashed under the couch to cower.

Though feeling momentarily bad for scaring Heidi, I just couldn't stop doing all the things terribly excited people tend to do. As I boogied past the phone, I snatched it up and dialed the one person I knew who would be celebrating this victory in much the same way, if he was aware of the situation and, of course, awake.

The phone rang about a dozen times before he answered it. I heard a loud thud followed by some scraping noises. I pictured the phone hitting the carpeted floor and dangling a bit before being picked up again. The mumbled greeting, "Uhhh. Hullo," sounded like it had been filtered through a pillow.

I had to laugh at my old friend. "Hey Austin, it's Jay. Y'know, if you had an answering machine, you'd still be sleeping."

"Ugh. I am still sleeping."

Another hearty chuckle escaped me. "So man, what're ya doing for the next week?"

"Huh?"

"Dude," I continued, "I won a Crazy Climber arcade machine. I finally got us one!"

Austin Ridenour's long pause made me wonder, was he processing the information, or had he fallen back asleep? It being two o'clock in the afternoon, his sleep-soggy brain probably wanted another hour or two of rest. "Mmph. Uh. Crazy Climber, you say? Sweet. How'd ya manage that, Jay?"

"Oh my friend, how do you think I found it?"

I could practically hear Austin's smile as he spoke. "Ya haven't kicked that eBay addiction yet, huh? There's gotta be a twelve step program in place by now."

"You crack me up, little buddy!" I said, adding, "If I had booted the habit, I wouldn't have been able to purchase Crazy Climber for the low, low price of three hundred and ten dollars."

After another loud clunk and a bit more shuffling and scuffling, Austin said, "Sorry, I keep droppin' the phone. Anyway, three hundred bucks? Man, that sounds cheap. Is it one of the cocktail table models?"

"Nope, it's a full-sized, upright arcade cabinet."

He yawned into the phone before replying. "Huh. I would've easily guessed double that price."

"I know, right? It was a perfect storm of a slightly damaged cabinet, a newbie seller and an auction ending in the middle of the day. I had to call in sick..." I paused to cough twice for dramatic effect, "to assure my place in front of the computer."

"Oh, you filthy liar! So, does that include shipping?"

I had to smile, even though I really didn't know how this would play out. "No, and that, Austy my friend, leads me ever so daintily back to my original inquiry. The game is in a small city in Southern California. It's too big for UPS, so it would have to be shipped with a freight company. This means it would be crammed in the back of a huge semi, which could take weeks to get here, would jack up the price astronomically and may very well arrive as a pile of circuit boards and kindling."

Austin had finally removed enough sleep from his brain to get the gears flowing. "So, what Jay, you want me to go to California and get it?"

"No, doofus, I want us to go get it. I have vacation time coming up, you're an unemployed slug and I'm pretty sure I can get us a truck."

"I'm not a slug. I'm more of a sloth. Slugs don't sleep the afternoon away."

"Touché. So again I ask you, what are you doing next week?"

"Eh, not much, I guess. I reckon I could be sloth-like just as easily on the road as I could at home."

Grinning widely, I asked, "So you're in, then?"

He paused for a moment before answering. "Sure, why not? When do we leave?"

Grabbing my jacket while still cradling the phone precariously between my shoulder and left ear, I replied, "I'm coming over right now so we can plan our escape. Are you decent?"

"Dude, when have I ever been?"

"Good point. I'll be over in a few."

Pulling up the zipper on my windbreaker, I breathed a sigh of relief. If he'd have said no, I don't know what I would've done. I didn't have any other friends who would, or could, go off on a weeklong spur-of-the-moment adventure like this, and I definitely didn't have the gumption to go it alone. The very thought of leaving my comfort zone caused me more than a little trepidation, so having Austin along would make this possible for me. It would also be cool since we hadn't seen much of each other since he moved out.

Pulling into a crumbling concrete driveway off of Southgate Avenue, I started laughing softly to myself. Other than when I helped him move here, I had only visited this rented house one other time, back in the spring. Simply seeing the yard made me understand why he preferred coming to my place for our increasingly rare encounters. All of the grass had grown long enough to sprout seeds, and the yard sported several varieties of exotic weeds, some standing nearly as tall as my five-foot six-inch frame. However, the gigantic thistle bush impressed me the most. Growing up against the house, it looked dangerous with its massive prickers sticking out haphazardly, but its large purple flower on top gave it a surprisingly resplendent feel. I sidled around what appeared to be a small tree that had popped up in a sidewalk crack directly in front of the porch steps and rapped insistently upon the torn screen door. "Grass Cops, open up!"

Moments later, a pudgy, shirtless man pulled open the door part way, kicked at something on the other side of the door, then yanked it the rest of the way open. The fur-covered man with the disheveled black hair uttered, "Sorry Officer, I was gonna mow it today, but I've been called away on urgent business," as I eased past him and into his unkempt house.

In the couple months since I saw him last, Austin hadn't changed much. His hair hung a bit lower on his shoulders, and the small balding circle on top might've been a tad wider. The gut also might've expanded a smidgen as well, but fortunately I hadn't seen him shirtless in a long time, so I didn't have a proper frame of reference.

Looking around, I just couldn't help laughing. My buddy always had a packrat mentality. He literally could not throw out or sell anything, even hoarding the cardboard backing from notebook paper, for goodness sake! But in reality, anytime I needed anything, be it bubble wrap, cardboard boxes, even an empty tube from a roll of toilet paper, I knew Austin Ridenour would have it.

If I hadn't been here before, and known his lifestyle from our previous cohabitation, I would've assumed some sort of natural disaster had struck. The living room had piles, and what were probably piles before toppling, of books, clothes and papers of all kinds. DVDs and CDs, both in their boxes and naked, were strewn about the place on practically every horizontal surface. Some of the caseless CDs sat in stacks at least twenty high, coated with a noticeable layer of dust.

Also, had I not set foot in this place prior to now, I wouldn't have known the color of the carpeting in the living room. I literally could not see the floor through the stuff. "I love what you've done with the place," I said casually.

"Yeah, well," he replied with a wide grin as he picked up a presumably clean shirt from the floor to mercifully cover his rotund, grizzly-bear-hairy torso,

"I think the maid is pinned down in the kitchen. After a small avalanche in there a couple of days ago, I heard a pitiful squeal, but I haven't found the courage to go in and check."

I lowered my head and placed a hand to my heart. "Oh Consuelo, you will be missed." After knocking some stuff off of a chair and plopping down, I added, "All right buddy, so we'll need a game plan. First, do you have an atlas?"

Without hesitation, he walked over to one of his overflowing shelving units and stuck his hand in a seemingly random pile, about a third of the way down. He lifted up the junk and yanked out a large, slightly bent atlas. His house may have looked like a random conglomeration of junk, but I'd be willing to bet he could find almost anything. Austin always had a sharp mind. The dude did Calculus, for fun.

He dropped the atlas on top of a pile which I assumed had a coffee table under it somewhere, then bent over and snatched a balled-up sock from the floor. As he began kicking at the ground in search of its mate, he asked, "So tell me about this Crazy Climber you found. It's in Cali, huh?"

"Weedpatch, to be exact. It's a tiny little burg a bit south of Bakersfield. According to the auction text, it's been in a private collection most of its life. In fact, let's fire up your computer and I'll show it to ya."

Austin stuck his hand under the couch and retrieved his laptop. Setting it precariously on top of the debris field coffee table, he plugged it in and powered it up. Then he bent down and scooped up another wadded-up sock. "Oh hey, there ya are, ya little rascal!"

While we awaited the computer's boot-up sequence, Austin donned his newly found footwear and I tried not to shudder. "Okay," I said as I took control of the computer, "here we go. Take a gander."

The current owner of my Crazy Climber arcade machine claimed the two joysticks controlling the climbing motion were in perfect working order, tight and solid. The video screen looked unscathed, with no obvious burn-in from replaying the same scenes over and over, and the images of the building and the climber appeared to be sharp. This arcade classic had only one major problem, which kept the bidding low. The cabinet housing the monitor and circuit boards had a couple of deep grooves carved into the left side. "Well," Austin said, "I can see why the bidding didn't go higher."

"True, but really, the external damage doesn't bother me much. Most arcade game collectors demand perfection, but fortunately, I'm not most collectors."

Staring at the screen, I couldn't help but beam with pride. I now had my very own Crazy Climber. It, along with Galaga and Tempest, ranked as my three favorite arcade games. But Crazy had a unique dual joystick control scheme, so it didn't transfer well to the home market. While I had played versions of the other games on my Atari Jaguar or Austin's Sony Playstation, I couldn't play Crazy Climber anywhere but in the arcades. However, as the years passed by, the local arcades in and around Lansing, Michigan slowly phased the machine out of existence. "Hey, when do you think you last played Crazy?"

He thought for a moment before replying. "Boy, that's a tough one. The one at Aladdin's Castle broke down and never came back from repair. That was a long time ago. So, that means I played it last at Pinball Pete's. They got rid of theirs in, what, the late 80s, maybe as late as 1990? So, it's been at least a decade."

"That sounds about right for me, too. In fact, come to think of it, I was in East Lansing on New Year's Day 1990. Mark, Bill and I went to Pete's. I must've played it then. So this New Year's Eve, it'll be ten years. Whoa! Ten years." Suddenly, I felt kinda old.

"Well, that'll change soon enough, eh?"

"True that. Okay, so if you'll look at the atlas and plot us a course, I need to call work and see about time off."

"You don't have the time off yet? Oh, you crazy man." Tossing a thumb toward a pile in the corner, Austin added, "The phone's over there. Uh, third heap to the left."

"Under the pizza boxes?"

"That'd be my guess."

Shaking my head softly in mock disgust, I dug around in the pile, shifting several items until I located his old-school white rotary telephone. "Dude, I can't believe you've still got this relic. Isn't this like the one George Washington used?"

He shrugged. "Funny. It was actually Lincoln. He phoned in the Gettysburg Address with that thing. Anyway, I don't usually dial out with that one. I just use it for answering, if I can find it, of course. You can hear it ring all over the house. Besides, it's kinda cool and retro, don't ya think?"

"I suppose." I stared at the phone for a moment before continuing. "So buddy, have ya been looking for a job, or are you enjoying the carefree, sleep-all-day lifestyle of the unemployed?"

"Well, for your information, bub, I got a job a couple weeks ago."

My eyes popped wide open. "Really? Where at?"

"Downtown. It's a nighttime warehouse gig." Austin furrowed his brow when he said the word downtown. All those one-way streets and parallel parking really gave him fits.

"So, then why am I here? You can't go with me."

"Sure I can. I mean yeah, I could go to work tomorrow like my schedule says, but the way I see it, you just came along with a better offer."

Man, this guy rocks! "Really? You're quitting a job just for me?"

"Only if your name is Crazy Climber, and last I checked, you were still Jaymond Naylor, Esquire. Besides, I was gonna quit anyway. I hate pretty much everything about it. The people suck, the hours suck, the location sucks and the work, wait for it...it sucks. This way, I'll just stop showing up, they'll fire me and I can go back to collecting unemployment."

"Well, at least you have a plan. So why is this the first I'm hearing of it?"

Austin, who had wandered off into the kitchen, yelled, "Oh hey, I found Consuelo. Poor dear, I warned her not to mess with the giant stack of newspapers next to the fridge. That tiny woman never stood a chance. Anyway, it's not my fault we don't hang out more. Ya gotta admit, you haven't had much time for me since I moved out. Princess Bonnie takes up a lot of your time."

"It cracks me up you call her that. Oh, that reminds me, I need to call her before we leave." Though I hated to admit it, he had a point. My girlfriend didn't much care for Austin. Come to think of it, she didn't like most of my friends. "Okay, anyway, I'm calling work now, so shut your trap."

"Yes, master!"

As I dialed the number on his ancient rotary phone, being careful not to miss a number and have to start over, I felt the urge to say, "Dude, the last time I used one of these beasts was probably around the time I played Crazy last. You really got to..." When the switchboard operator greeted me, it dawned on me I hadn't formulated a plan. "Uh, hi. Bertha in HR, please."

After a few seconds of a Muzak version of Led Zeppelin's *Whole Lotta Love*, my supervisor Bertha Morris's startlingly masculine baritone voice assaulted me. "This is Bertha."

I coughed a couple of times before answering her, trying to reinforce the sickness angle I had alluded to in my earlier call. "Hi Bertha, this is Jay Naylor. Am I missing much today?"

"No, not really. Are you feeling any better?"

Though I didn't feel all that comfortable with dishonesty, I knew what I had to do. "A bit. Thanks for asking. Say Bertha, let me ask you something. How much notice does a person generally have to give before taking vacation time?" I really hoped she'd answer me before asking why.

"Why?"

Crap. "I need to take a week off. It's personal."

She paused for longer than I would've liked. After a few key clicks, she answered, "I see you have two weeks of vacation time coming to you. We normally need at least a two week notice, but we can waive it if it's for an emergency."

Somehow, I doubted driving to California to pick up a video game would constitute an emergency, so a lie shot out of my lips before I had thought it through. "My grandmother passed away. She lives in California. I need to pay my respects, y'know?"

Her normally deep voice softened considerably, and I think she even cooed. "Oh, you poor thing. I'm so sorry. What did she die of, if you don't mind me asking?"

"Um, gout. The gout finally did her in." Gout? Good Lord, why did that pop into my head? I knew nothing about gout. But, I put it out there, so I blathered on. "She battled it for years. We always said to her, 'Grandmama,' we called her that, y'know, 'Grandmama, you need to stop with all the rich foods. Put down the cheesecake. Stop eating all that ham!' But would she listen? No."

"I don't think ham causes gout, Jay."

"Uh, this was a rare form. Pork gout. I think all that bacon might've been a factor as well. I can't really say. I'm not a doctor. All I know is, the funeral is in three days and I feel I owe it to her to be there."

After another pause and some key clicks, Bertha replied, "Okay Jay, I have you down for a week of vacation. I'm sorry for your loss."

"Thanks, Bertha. Try not to miss me too much."

Snorting, she answered, "That's not going to be a problem."

Hanging up the phone, I exhaled heavily. "Okay, that's done."

"Pork gout, Jay?"

I turned to see Austin chowing down on a piece of boneless chicken. As a chunk of breading crumbled off and fell to the floor, I replied with a sheepish grin, "Yeah, that one surprised even me. But I guess she bought it."

"Okey-doke, then. And I've got the route plotted. What's next?"

"Now we need a truck. And I know just who to ask."

11

**TWO**

A mere two hours later, Austin and I stood in the house of our good buddy Phil Savage.

"Crazy Climber?" the tall, longhaired man asked with a puzzled expression. "I don't remember that game."

I furrowed my brow at him in disbelief. "Really? A little guy in a green jumpsuit, climbing up a building one window at a time. No?"

Austin added, "Women tossing flowerpots at your head, birds trying to crap on you? You really don't remember it?"

Phil's shrug gave me my answer. "Ya think I'd remember a game featuring bird poop. Oh well, I guess I'll play it soon enough. And it's in sunny California?"

"Indeed," I replied. "Since your pickup is vehicle number two in your driving repertoire, I was hoping you wouldn't mind lending it to us."

His smile faded, which wasn't the best of signs. Then he gave us a good sign by walking over to his key chain, and snatching it up off the kitchen counter. "Jay," he began slowly, staring blankly at the key, "you know I'd give up my right nut for you, but the truck, she's been my baby for years."

"Okay dude," Austin chimed in, "lend us your nut and we'll drive that there instead. What kinda mileage does it get?"

After a decent chuckle, I said, "Phil, buddy, you know we'll take good care of it. The truck, I mean. We'll feed her premium if you like."

He removed the key from the chain and held it at arm's length. "Actually, my main concern is her age. Ol' Red doesn't do much traveling anymore."

I couldn't help but laugh at that. "Ol' Red? You call your truck Ol' Red?"

"I do. Why, you think that's funny?" Phil's face displayed no levity.

"Oh, uh, no, not at all. After all, I call my car Ol'... green."

Clearly not amused, he continued. "Just remember, ya need to give her frequent breaks."

I plucked the key from his grasp. "Hey my friend, if it makes ya happy, we'll stop every five miles."

"That won't be necessary, fellas. Just treat her with care."

As I stared at his key, a thought struck me. I dug into my pocket and pulled out my house key. "Oh, that reminds me, can you possibly watch my house and feed my cat? I'll let ya play Crazy for free."

He took the key from my hand and set it on the counter. "You'd let me play for free anyway. But yes,

I'll keep Heidi alive for you. As long as you do the same for Ol' Red."

"You got a deal," I gave Phil a smile and a handshake.

Between the two of us, we realized we only had around five hundred in cash. I had the money for the arcade game safely tucked away in my duffel bag, and my remaining ninety dollars in my wallet, along with my lone credit card. Austin had his hundred bucks stuffed in his sock, or maybe some place I didn't want to think about, but no credit card. He always told me he didn't believe in credit cards, but I always surmised the credit card companies didn't believe in him.

Austin shook his head slowly. "Man, we don't have much cash, do we?"

"Nah, not really. Kinda pathetic for a couple of thirty-year-old guys. I guess neither of us are very good at saving money, huh?"

"True. But when it comes down to it, I want what I want."

"I know. I'm the same way. I mean, I have some money in my savings account, but I really don't want to touch that. Besides, I plan on charging as much as possible. It'll be fine. With gas being around a buck a gallon, the fuel cost won't be our main concern."

Austin corrected me. "Actually, last I checked, it was closer to a dollar ten."

"Eh, either way, it won't kill us. And I plan on charging the gas as well." Flashing him a confident grin, I decided to repeat myself. "Don't worry. It'll be fine."

Before beginning our journey, Austin gazed at the map for maybe five seconds, jabbing at it with his right index finger. "Okay, to get outta Lansing, we have options. How 'bout we go 69 to 65 to 40."

"Hut hut hut," I said, trying to make a stupid football joke. Austin stared at me like I had just spoken the Declaration of Independence in Swahili, so I quickly added, "What sights will we see going that way?"

Austin shrugged. "I dunno, really. We're going from Indianapolis to Nashville and on to Weedpatch. We can go a different route on the way home. But this way, we get to drive straight through the heart of redneck country. That oughta be good fer a hoot, I plumb reckon."

I laughed half-heartedly, even though it wasn't any funnier than my joke.

We figured our best bet would be to get to sleep early and start fresh in the morning, so I gave Austin a choice. He could either sleep on my couch or leave his front door unlocked. I knew from experience he would have difficulty getting to sleep early, and I would have to roust him to get him motivated. Since he didn't care for either option, he compromised by giving me a key to his house. As I dropped him off at home, I said, "Go to bed early. I'll be here by sunrise." He grimaced noticeably, but nodded his agreement.

I woke up bright and early the next morning, feeling refreshed and ready for the long drive ahead. Trying to give Austin as much rest as possible, I waited until nine o'clock before heading over.

Walking into his cluttered domicile, I headed straight for his bedroom. As I approached, I could hear his three alarms beeping in cacophonous unity, nearly drowned out by my buddy's tumultuous snoring. Oh yes, Austin's snore could wake the dead. Though I did miss having him at my place, I did not miss the noise. Never in my life had I heard such a racket emanating from a human being. Even down the hall and through our closed bedroom doors, I would be jolted awake from time to time. "Man," I muttered to no one, "I am not gonna get much sleep this week. I shoulda bought some earplugs."

It took three attempts, spaced about ten minutes apart, to pull him to consciousness. After he grabbed a quick shower and a bite to eat, we hit the road.

The first leg of our journey started off smoothly enough. As we headed out of Lansing on Interstate 69, I took the wheel. We saw sparse traffic headed south, so it gave us plenty of time to chat. I turned to gaze at my friend, who had his head propped against the side window. As a snort of a snore emanated from him, I elbowed him sharply in the arm.

Snorting again as he popped awake, he shot me a cross expression. "Dude, I had to get up early, remember?"

"Yeah I know, but it's far too soon for you to subject me to that buzzsaw snore of yours. I'll hear enough of that when I'm lying there trying to sleep." I wracked my brain trying to conjure up a bit of simple conversation. "So Austy, how long've we been friends?"

He shrugged. "We met in middle school, became friends in ninth grade. It'll be twenty years come next year."

"Sounds about right, twenty years in 2000. So, hey, whatdya think about this whole Y2K thing? Is the Millennium Bug gonna cause the end of the world?"

"Man, I sure hope so!"

I shot him a queer look. "Whatdya mean, you hope so?"

"We've been hearing the hype for months, years really, all the crap about computers crashing, banks and the government losing all our records, etc. Some worst-case scenarios have nuclear codes resetting and power grids failing. End of the world stuff."

"Uh, yeah. Sounds frightening."

A sinister grin crept onto Austin's scruffy face. "You kidding? Sounds fantastic, man! Well, not the threat of a nuclear winter mind you, but the no more debt, and especially the no more society part, really appeals to me. Anarchy rules!" He threw his fist in the air for emphasis.

"Yeah, but Austin, under this scenario, computers would stop working. You love computers."

My buddy shrugged. "Eh, I'll read books. I love books as much as I love computers. But I really love the irony of it all. Computers were designed to make our lives better, but due to a tiny programming issue, using two-digit year codes instead of four, the world will come crashing down around us. It's fun, man!"

"Fun," I said softly. "The end of civilization sounds like fun to you." I rolled my eyes.

"Sure thing! You see where the world's headed. It's only a matter of time before the American Empire collapses under its own weight. We're just like Rome. All dynasties fail eventually. I've just always hoped to be alive to see it, to have a front-row seat to Armageddon."

I couldn't help staring at him for a moment, my mouth agape. "I had no idea you felt this way."

"You know I think people are morons, as a general rule. This is an offshoot of that. The idea that some idiots, who fancied themselves intelligent eggheads, designed all the world's computer programs with such a tiny yet fatal flaw. It's such a great irony, y'know?"

Sometimes, I found it hard to tell the difference between serious and joking with him. I suspect he offered a bit of both in this conversation. "Huh. Well personally, I don't think anything's gonna happen, but I don't feel right joking about it."

He laughed out loud at my comment. "Like verbally walking under a ladder, is it Jay?"

"Kinda, I guess."

"Either way, my friend, we'll know what's what in about six months. Just in case," he added, "I'm buying extra water and bullets. Oh, and I'm not getting you a Christmas present."

"Well, you could get me water for Christmas. Or bullets."

He put his finger to the side of his nose as his smile widened. "Nice. Always thinkin'!"

We had no fun getting through Indianapolis, as it seemed like a thousand expressways converged around that city. But we eventually ambled our way onto I-65, heading south toward Nashville.

Not too long after maneuvering through the Indianapolis quagmire, I had some time to think. I had this nagging feeling I had forgotten to do something.

Mentally, I ran through my checklist. *Okay, I have the directions and the money. I have the seller's home and work phone number. Why, I even have the number to his fancy cell phone. The lucky sod. I've always wanted a cell phone, but I don't have a real need, and besides, who but a rich dude can afford one? Never mind that. Focus. I have Phil watching my place and he promised to feed and water the cat. I called work. I still can't believe Bertha fell for that. Dang, she's as gullible as my girlfriend. Why...*

"Crap!" I yelled loud enough to jolt Austin awake. Not an easy feat, to be sure.

"Aaahh! Whassup?"

"Oh man, I completely forgot to call Bonnie! Here I am halfway to Cali and I didn't even tell my girl I was leaving. Cripes, she's gonna kill me."

"Eh," Austin responded with a dismissive wave, "don't worry about it. I doubt she'll even notice you're gone. If I were you, I wouldn't even bother calling. Show up in a week and play it off."

Spoken like a divorced man. Austin had been understandably bitter about women since his wife left him a few years ago. I still found it hard to believe she called his snoring 'Cruel and Unusual Punishment' in the divorce papers. Or was it 'Mental Cruelty?' Either way, I know his snore sounded like a lumberjack with a malfunctioning chainsaw, but it being grounds for a separation? A pair of earplugs would've been cheaper, if she had so chosen. No, there had to be more to it, but Austin never wanted to speak about it. We've talked about everything else, from the lackluster Detroit Tigers to the end of the world, but not that. We may be best friends, but I had no desire to pry, to open up that can of creamed corn. I always assumed he would talk about it in his own time.

I spent the next several miles worrying about my situation, trying to decide what to say to Bonnie. When we pulled in to a truck stop to refuel, I hightailed it to the nearest pay phone.

Her phone rang the prerequisite four times before her answering machine kicked in. Breathing a sigh of relief, I realized I now wouldn't have to deal with her directly. "Hi honey, it's me. Say, funny story. I'm, uh, on my way to California right now. I'm driving with Austin as we speak. I'll be back by Monday. I'll give..."

She chose that moment to pick up the phone and berate me. "You're driving to California? What on Earth for? If you're taking a vacation, don't you think I might've wanted to go too? I have time saved up, and you know I have family in San Diego. Typical, just typical. Only thinking of yourself."

She has family in San Diego? Huh. I don't remember her ever mentioning that. I decided now was not the optimal time to bring it up. "Oh, hey

Bonnie. Uh, yeah, we're driving there in Phil's truck to pick up a Crazy Climber arcade game."

"A what? A game? You're driving three thousand miles for a stupid game?"

"Um, yeah, Crazy Climber. It's not stupid. Well okay, it's a little stupid, but..."

"You're darn right it's stupid. And how much did you pay for this game?"

"Oh, I got a great deal. Just three hundred bucks."

She sighed audibly. Man, I hated that sigh of hers, like an airy slap of disappointment. "My God Jay, no wonder you never have any money saved up. Always spending it on stupid toys. You're never going to grow up, are you?"

"What? I..."

"Look. I wasn't planning on doing it this way, but I may as well. I think it's time we started seeing other people."

"What? What are you talking about? When I get back..."

"No," she yelled, "it's over, Jay. We've been dating for nearly a year. In that time, I've gotten a better job with two promotions, a house with a back yard and a brand new car. You, you spend all your disposable income on video games and computer equipment, and other childish stuff. You need to grow up. You're over thirty, Jay. You're still the same nerdy boy you were in high school. Become an adult, already. Think about others, think about your future, and not just immediate gratification."

"Oh, that's just not true. I've always said immediate gratification takes too long. You..."

"Good Lord." She assaulted me with another sharp sigh. "You never take things seriously. I'm breaking up with you, and you're making lame jokes."

"They're not that lame," I said softly.

"Goodbye, Jay." With that final sentence, she hung up.

Setting the handset down, I whispered, "Whoa."

I slowly shuffled over to the truck with my head drooping. Austin stood leaning up against the front grill, munching on a Snickers bar. Through caramelly breath he asked, "So, how is Princess Bonnie?"

My sigh was much softer than Bonnie's, like a fleeting summer breeze. "Oh, well, she kinda dumped me."

"Harsh. She that mad you left without telling her?"

"I guess it was the final straw."

"Told ya not to call her." Slapping me on the back, he walked past me and tossed the wrapper in the trash. "Eh, don't worry. When we get back, you can talk to her, flash her that smile of yours, say something witty, and she'll be putty again. So let's get rollin' already."

As I climbed into the truck, I highly doubted his take on the situation. But still, I couldn't do a thing about it now, so I may as well take his optimism to heart. Why not, right?

At around midnight, we approached the city of Nashville. We had stopped a couple times en route, but not much more than a quick meal, some gas and a pee, then back on the road again. Okay, I know we promised Phil we would stop constantly, but dang, our excitement could barely be contained. Besides, Ol' Red didn't seem to be having any trouble. This was a good thing, since neither of us had very much mechanical inclination. Based upon our respective automotive experiences, Austin probably had a bit more acumen than I did. After all, he spent a bit of his youth standing in the garage with his father, handing him tools. Not that he paid a lot of attention, but at least he had that much. At least he knew what tools looked like.

On the other side of the spectrum, my dad had a different mentality, which I inherited: Drive it until it died, leave it smoldering by the side of the road and hitchhike or walk home. Basically, this meant I had blown up a lot of car engines in my youth, and walked many miles on the highway. It might've been my imagination, but it seemed like no matter how far away I got, I could still see the smoke plume off in the distance, as if to wave a final goodbye.

Dad's philosophy followed me through my first few cars, starting with the 1980 baby blue Ford Mustang I inherited from the folks. Actually, the Mustang turned out to be a good first car in that it clearly had a strong urge to live. Clinging tenaciously to life, it survived quite a while despite all of my negligence. I once had a mechanic at the Jiffy Lube tell me he didn't feel right charging me full price for the oil change, since the engine didn't actually have any oil in it. He said he pulled the plug and nothing came out. I drove that car until it threw a piston, or something. All I knew for sure was, it had a gaping hole in the engine, and in the hood.

From there, I destroyed several more cars in seemingly rapid succession, from a crappy blue Chevy Nova, whose engine exploded in a fiery mess, to the rusty old LTD I drove for five months until the engine seized up due to – surprise, surprise – lack of oil. Why, I even owned and eviscerated a very used Volkswagen Rabbit. Then, I bought my first new car, a Saturn, and learned about something called preventive maintenance.

So, Austin had a basic understanding of car tools, and I brought to the table a lot of experience staring at smoking automotive remains while rubbing my chin thoughtfully.

Once in Nashville, we drove around in search of the cheapest-looking lodging we could find, preferably with a bar and restaurant close by. We realized a couple hundred bucks would not get us a lot of four star rooms, so we decided to 'dive' it.

As we turned on to Wedgehill Avenue, a building with peeling paint and orange shrubbery caught our attention. This place had what we needed, with the motel and bar conveniently connected into one monstrously ugly façade. The place had the name Bob's Snoozers Motel adorning the top half of a faded yellow plastic sign. I believe the lower portion read The Spewing Tourist, but with at least one bulb burned out on that part, I couldn't be sure. Okay, it actually had Bob's Country Palace on the sign, but allow me a little artistic freedom here.

After securing a room at Bob's, settling in and startling the cockroaches, we decided to check out the adjoining restaurant/bar. As we entered the establishment, we felt a bit out of our element. Now, neither Austin nor myself were much into the bar scene, but at least in good old Lansing, Michigan, the bars appeared relatively clean and safe. Here, we feared stopping for too long in any one spot, thinking our shoes might become cemented to the sticky floor, coated with beer and Lord knows what else. We sprinted over to a vacant table and plopped down. Then, after my butt got stuck to the hard wooden chair, I peeled myself loose and we chose another table.

We counted around thirty people at Bob's, some playing pool, others hacking away at the couple of old video games in the corner, two skuzzy-looking dudes playing darts, and the rest sitting at the bar drinking their lives away.

The waitress, a tall, surly-looking woman who appeared to be in her late 40s, slowly walked over to our table. She had dishwater blonde hair and a cigarette dangling from her mouth. "So what'll ya have?"

This seemed a bit odd. "Well, we haven't seen a menu yet."

She looked at me like I was the stupidest person on the planet. "Look Mac, this ain't no dinin' experience. Ya want a burger and fries or don't ya?"

I snickered, which caused her to shoot me a particularly dirty glare. So I replied, "Sure, that's fine. And how about a rum and Coke?"

She shook her head slowly as she left, not even allowing Austin to order anything. She came back a minute later with two bottles of Lodestone beer, half-dropping them on the table. "I've had a really lousy day," she said matter-of-factly, "so deal with these while your burgers are cooking, okay?"

"Fair enough," Austin said with a fake smile.

"The customer's never right," I muttered under my breath.

Austin, who didn't care much for beer, shocked me when he grabbed his and greedily downed about half of it. He shook his upper body in a spasm, the way a person does after swallowing some nasty tasting cough syrup. "Ew. Might as well make the best of it, eh?" With that, he picked up his rotund frame and trudged over to the video games. He dug a quarter out of his pocket, and started playing Galaga. The sight of a Galaga machine in a place like this, so many miles from home, made me smile. Seemed like every bar in the world had that game, and we were probably two of the best players in Lansing. Since people didn't play it much anymore, we could both easily get on the high score board back home at Pinball Pete's, or one of the several bars in town that still had it.

While my dark-haired friend played away, I slowly scanned the crowd. Now, I generally tried my best not to stereotype people, but being only human and having lived my whole life in the same town, I couldn't help categorizing this bar as redneck. The Randy Travis blaring from the jukebox added nicely to that ambiance, as did the guy who, after he lost a game of pool, started pounding on the winner's face.

Even though I didn't much fancy beer myself, I found mine going down pretty quickly and smoothly. We hadn't had anything to eat or drink in hours, and after being on the road, this felt kinda cool. I finished my beer and got another one. Being a small, skinny dude, weighing a buck-thirty on a fat day, I already felt a nice little buzz, thanks to my empty stomach.

As I continued to survey the populace, I noticed a striking young woman staring at me. She sent a sly little grin my way. This tiny woman, probably not even five foot tall, easily held the title of 'prettiest thing in this dump.' Her high cheekbones really turned me on, as did her auburn hair, playfully cascading over her shoulders, ending mid-way down her back. Holding my gaze, she stood up but had to take a moment to steady herself before gliding in my direction. *Ooo, pretty and drunk. I like her already!* She was a pure pleasure to watch as she moved her svelte body toward me. "Howdy!" Though she had to shout to be heard over the jukebox, she still, somehow, whispered seductively. "Ya mind if I sit, baby?"

Mind, hell! "Not at all," I said, trying to sound all suave by lowering my voice an octave. "I'm Jay. What's your name, honey?"

She sat and put her hand on my leg, using the grip to slide her chair closer to mine. "Mindy. Where ya from, and where ya going?"

I told her all about our little journey, and although I could tell she didn't really care, she listened half-heartedly as she moved her hand slowly up and down my thigh. After a couple more minutes of mindless chatter on my part, she asked if I had a room in the area. When I replied in the affirmative, she leaned right up to my ear and whispered, "Well then Jay, what are we waitin' fer?"

When her tongue nicked the edge of my ear, and I felt her hand on my backside, I had no idea what we were waiting for. Well, I guess Bonnie dumping me a few hours ago turned out to be a blessing in disguise. Not being the kind of guy who would ever cheat on his woman, this wouldn't be happening had I not remembered to call. It was odd how life worked sometimes, and my mind tried to dredge up that old saying about closing doors and opening windows.

*Bah, what'm I doing thinking about this crap?* I glanced up at the back of Austin's head before turning back to her. "Just wait here, little lady. I gotta tell my buddy not to wait up."

She winked as she slowly slid her hand off my butt, keeping it under the table as she gave me that sly smile again. I stood up slowly. (I wanted to stand up fast, but I had a couple things working against me.) I marched over to my friend, still working over the Galaga machine. "Hey Austy, how ya scorin'?"

"Doing good, man," he replied, not taking his eyes off the swirling invaders. "Still got another ship after this one, and just look at the points!"

Not surprisingly, he already had the high score. "Speaking of scoring," I said, nearly giggling like a schoolgirl, "I got a hot chick who wants to go back to the room. So I'll see ya later, okay?"

Short of a bomb threat, very little could wrench Austin's eyes from a video game screen. He turned completely around to look toward our table. "Who, that surly old waitress?"

I reared back to smack him as I spun my head toward the table. The only person over there was, in fact, the waitress with our burgers. My heart sank, not to mention something else, as I quickly scanned the room. Crap, the stunning lady had vanished on me. "Oh, man! Maybe she's in the bathroom." I said dejectedly as I shuffled back to claim my dinner.

"That'll be seven-fifty," the waitress blurted out as I arrived at the table.

As I reached into my back pocket for my wallet, I asked, "Ya didn't happen to see an auburn haired woman leave the table, did ya?"

"I didn't see nuthin, Mac. Seven-fifty."

With my hand touching the spot where my wallet normally resided, I began to panic when I didn't feel the usual bump. My eyes widened and I felt my face turn pale! "What the hell? My wallet!"

Doing a complete 360, I spun around rapidly, as if I could somehow see my own posterior if I revolved quickly enough. I scanned the table and floor, and back toward Austin, but I didn't see it. Then I remembered exactly where Mindy had put her hand earlier, and I knew a pretty face had suckered me. "Seriously, you didn't see a woman, real short with long, reddish-brown hair, said her name was Mindy?"

The waitress actually laughed as she dropped the burger plates on the table. "You men are soooo stupid! I'll be back in a minute to get the money. Maybe you better go sweet talk someone yourself, Mac." She chuckled her way back toward the bar.

I ambled over to Austin, who fought valiantly to avoid losing his last life. Ultimately, the alien swarm won out, like it always did. "Game over," he said aloud to no one in particular, "high score on the screen." As he finished entering his initials, A.I.R., into the machine, he turned to me and recognized, but slightly misread, my countenance. "So, she bolted on ya, eh?"

"That's not the half of it! That chick stole my wallet!"

It always amazed me how Austin took most things in stride, except perhaps losing at a video game or, apparently, the end of the world. "That sucks, dude," he said fairly nonchalantly as we moseyed back to the table. Then, his eyes widened in panic as well. "That wasn't our Crazy Climber money, was it?"

"Thank God, no. I stuffed that in my bag before we left. But it's all my spending cash, and the credit card, not to mention my license." I continued to scan the bar, clearly a losing proposition.

Just then, the waitress came back and did something that made me want to kiss her. Well, almost. She plopped my wallet on the table. As I excitedly reached for it, she said, "Don't bother looking for money or credit cards, them's history. She had no use for your ugly mug on that license or this cheap, fake leather wallet, so she dropped it in the parking lot. Someone found it out there and brought it in." She looked at Austin and held out her hand. "Seven-fifty, buddy. I don't have all day."

I started to chastise her. "This wallet's hemp, not cheap leather. It's..." But I quickly stopped. No one cared, least of all me.

Austin paid for our food and we sat in relative silence, chewing away at overdone burgers and squishy fries. By relative silence, I mean Austin kept rambling on and on about something, but I paid him no mind. I spent my time quietly brooding, splitting my thoughts between anger and embarrassment. The idea that some skanky siren could saunter up to me and relieve me of not only my money, but also my dignity, it fired me up something fierce. But at the same time, I felt all eyes upon me, as if to say, "Oh, look at that idiot. He let some woman steal his wallet." Being shy by nature, I've always hated being the center of attention. The negative context made it that much worse.

So, as we sat there eating, Austin blathered on and on while I quietly seethed. He probably figured he'd help me by trying to take my mind off the situation. Finally, when he asked me a pointed question and I failed to respond, he reached over and flicked the tip of my nose. "Hey!" I shot him an angry glare.

"Just getting your attention. Look Jay, we both know this sucks. We've lost our safety net. Neither of us have a credit card now. But I still have my cash. We'll be okay. We just can't be extravagant anymore."

Okay, that made me chortle out loud. "Oh no, you mean we can't afford to eat at high-end dining establishments like this one? How will my delicate palate adjust?"

"It'll be a challenge, dude. But we'll make it."

"Sure, easy for you to say. You've got that layer of fat to live off of."

Austin reached over and flicked my nose again. "Man, shut up!"

Once we staggered over to the motel, Austin fell fast asleep. Damn, I knew better than to let Snore Master 2000 get to dream land before me. As I lay there, listening to the demon in the next bed, I tried to put the events of the day out of my mind. But no, I just couldn't stop dwelling on it. I think the worst part was feeling like I had no real recourse. I wanted to do something, but nothing seemed to make sense. Number one, I should go to the cops in the morning and file a report. But did I really want to waste time doing that? Besides, what would I tell them, a short, auburn-haired woman stole my money? I knew nothing more about her. Would that delay our departure? Would we be forced to stay in Nashville? And what if they found her? Would I have to return for the trial? Man, I never want to come back here again. I hate this beer-drinking, country-music-blaring, pickpocket-filled city.

A big part of me simply wanted to forget this ever happened, take it as a life lesson and never again let another pretty woman put her hand on my derriere without an invite. Maybe I should get one of those wallets with the biker chain attached to my belt loop. I wondered if they even made biker chains for hemp wallets. It sounded mighty contradictory.

However, I knew I needed to cancel the credit card in the morning. I must remember that.

Okay, I forced myself to turn off my brain and stop thinking. I rolled over onto my stomach, crammed the pillow over the top of my head in an attempt to drown out the snoring, and finally, gratefully, I fell asleep.

FOUR

The next morning, we packed up our belongings, swiped a couple towels and some cockroaches and checked our money. My duffel bag still held the Crazy Climber cash, and we had a little less than seventy dollars of Austin's money. Thank God I charged the room and filled up the tank before I lost the card.

Austin reacted in a very cool manner over the whole ordeal. He could have bitched at me, but it wasn't his style. Frankly, it amazed me he didn't outright laugh at me.

Hitting the road fairly early that morning, we found the I-40 expressway with relative ease and started our westward trek toward Weedpatch.

I had spent the last forty-five minutes staring out the passenger window at the constantly moving landscape, not really focusing on any of the sights as they flew by. Turning to look at Austin, I became a bit concerned at the droopiness of his eyelids. Fearing this as a possible harbinger of a bad situation, I uttered, "Are we there yet?"

When he barely responded, I knew I had to do something to jar him awake, so I quickly punched him in the arm. He looked at me with venom in his eyes. "Ow! What the hell?"

"Slug Bug."

"I beg your pardon?"

"I just saw a VW bug."

"So?"

"If I see one, I get to punch you in the arm."

Looking both angry and confused, he asked, "Why?"

"It's a game."

He continued to glare at me until an evil grin crept upon his face. "Okay fine. I'll play along. The next time I see pavement, I'll punch you in the face. Oh look, pavement."

As he balled up his fist and cocked his arm back, I quickly yelped, "Okay, you win. No Slug Bug."

"Uh-huh. That's what I thought."

Sighing, I returned my gaze to my window. Without looking over at him, I said, "Man, I'm bored. We gotta do something. We could do the license plate game."

"Okay." In one rapid motion, he slugged me in the arm. "I saw a plate."

"Ow. That's not how you play. We're done with the punching."

He whacked my arm one more time. "Now we're done with the punching. And by the way, I'm alert now, so thanks."

Being much poorer, we tried our best to drive straight through to California, which honestly turned out to be impossible. We survived on vending machine junk food and water all the way past Amarillo, Texas, but even taking turns driving and dozing, we both became really fatigued and had to stop for the night in the border town of Glenrio.

We thought the last place we stopped at was a dive. This motel looked so bad that even the cockroaches we swiped from Nashville took one look at the room and skedaddled, snickering amongst themselves. But frankly, we knew we wouldn't find a place that charged less than this hole, so we reluctantly took our chances staying at the Route 30 Motel. We found the name rather queer, since we were on I-40. It lowered our opinion of this place another notch.

Walking across the parking lot and down the street a block or so, we came upon a bar called the Prairie Rat Saloon. It either had a dirt floor or a very dirty floor. Neither of us had the inclination to get down there and check. We sat at the bar and decided to splurge on burgers and water. The bartender gave us water drinkers a foul look, but I think he felt better when he served our tap water in dirty glasses.

"So Austy, another day'll get us to Weedpatch."

"Yup," he replied as he scanned the room, "but we'll probably get there in the middle of the night. We'll hafta camp out in his driveway 'til morning."

"Hopefully, it'll be dry. I'll sleep in the back. You can take the cab. After all, it's my fault we're in this predicament."

Austin paid little attention to me. He spotted, in this fairly empty bar, the usual row of arcade games, and among them, the seemingly omnipresent Galaga. "Well, look what they got here. I wonder if we'll see Galaga at every place we stop?"

"I wouldn't be surprised. If a place wants a video game in the corner, it's an easy choice. Everybody's heard of it, everybody loves it. It's easy to play, difficult to master."

Leaping to his feet, Austin pulled out a ten-dollar bill and tossed it on the counter. "That's for food. You know where I'm going."

I wanted to complain, but hell, at least he had money to blow. Besides, this cheap entertainment only cost a quarter or two.

He marched up to the machine, and observed a local guy finishing up a particularly crappy game. Only on the sixth level, he tried in vain not to lose his last ship. Even from my seat several feet away, I could see Austin holding in his laughter. The man, wearing the standard issue cowboy hat and boots with his white button-down shirt, squirmed around like mad, as if body English would somehow translate into a better maneuvering ship. It didn't. When his ship exploded at the end of the level, he spewed a few expletives and shot an angry glare at his buddy, standing next to him leaning up against a pinball machine. Then, he noticed Austin behind him with a quarter in his hand and a grin on his face. "Yew problee think yew kin do better, don'tchew, boy?"

Austin, not always thinking before opening his mouth, said matter-of-factly, "Uh Yah! My dead grandmother could do better."

The guy, a couple inches shorter than Austin's five-foot six-inch frame, took only one step to the side, not leaving enough room for Austin's husky physique to squeak by. As Austin pushed his way past, the guy said, "Bet yew think yew could beat me in this here game, huh fat boy?"

Austin looked at him and let loose with a loud chuckle. "In my sleep, pal. See that high score?" He pointed to the score of 150,630 that adorned the top of the screen. "I can top that without breaking a sweat."

The tiny cowboy turned and yelled to a man sitting a couple tables away, "Hey Dwayne, this Twinkie sez he kin beat yer high score!"

I heard this just as I took a huge bite of my burger, and almost spat the congealing mouthful at the bartender. I watched as the guy stood up. And up. And up. To say he loomed large was a mild understatement, kinda like saying the Grand Canyon was a pretty decent-sized hole. He sauntered slowly over to Austin and spoke very slowly and in a deep baritone voice, "I'll bet ya fifty bucks I can beat ya."

It didn't come across as a request, more like the statement, "We are betting, and that is that." I stood up and took a couple of steps toward the group, but before I could get close enough to say anything to my friend, he stated, "You're on, Gargantua. You wanna go first?"

Big Man stood arrow-straight, jabbing a meaty finger at the screen. Austin shrugged, tossed in the quarter and proceeded to have himself a fine game, topping the guy's high score by a bit. Pointing at the new high score of 187,220, he turned and beamed at the crowd that had gathered around the machine. Then, after flashing the same cocky grin at the big guy and the little guy, he tossed me a nod and a wink.

The behemoth, with no discernable emotion, rested his left hand gently on Austin's right shoulder. He patted it a couple of times like the top of a dog's head, then used his right hand to punch my buddy solidly in the stomach. Not surprisingly, this evaporated the grin from Austin's face. When he doubled over and hit the floor, gasping and wheezing like an asthmatic, Dwayne calmly slipped in front of the machine, slid in his quarter and began playing. Pushing my way through the crowd, I crouched down next to my friend. At his insistence, I helped him to his feet so he could watch the action.

Turned out Dwayne played a pretty mean game as well, even though he did lose two ships pretty early on, giving the recovering Austin a reason to start smiling again. But once he found a groove, the big man just kept playing and playing, going through several levels without losing another ship. When his last ship exploded in a puff of blue smoke, the machine had a new high score up top of 194,480. He had beaten my friend at his own game, so to speak.

Dwayne slowly pivoted around to leer at Austin, a satisfied grin spreading across his rugged face. Not uttering a word, the big man simply held out his right hand, palm up, and continued to smile as the rest of the crowd cheered loudly.

We quickly finished our food and drinks and vacated the premises. As we shuffled out of that horrible place, their laughter and mocking was palpable even after the door slammed shut.

As we made our way back to the room, I turned and yelled, "What in the hell were you thinking, Austin?"

"Don't start with me."

"But c'mon, fifty bucks! You know we..."

Austin turned sharply, grabbed both my shoulders and spun me to put us eye-to-eye. "I said stop. I didn't harp on you for your stupid move. It's done. Drop it." With that out of his mouth, he gave me a slight shove, turned and stormed into the motel room.

I stood there for a moment before entering, kinda wishing I smoked cigarettes. Now would've been a

prime opportunity for a reason to linger outside. But
instead of polluting my lungs, I simply leaned up
against the truck for a spell. Staring up at the full
moon, I crossed my arms, attempting to ward off the
slight chilliness of a summer night in Texas. As a
couple of high, puffy clouds slowly drifted past, I had
to wonder if we had any money left.

After about fifteen minutes of cloud gazing, I
entered our room. I could hear the shower splattering
water into the tub, so I decided to climb into my bed
and attempt to fall asleep.

I really wanted to scream, yell and even smack the
crap out of Austin, but seeing how he didn't do that to
me with my monetary mishap, I bit my tongue hard
enough to pop it off and leave it in the dirt of that
nasty bar's parking lot. At least in losing my money, I
didn't get physically abused. Poor guy.

I didn't have any luck falling asleep before Austin
emerged from the bathroom. Without a word, he
ambled over to his bed and plopped down.

Hours later, I had counted all the dots in the ceiling
tiles. Since I didn't hear any snoring, I knew sleep was
avoiding Austin's brain as well as mine. As we both
lay awake, I softly asked him if we had any money left
at all. "Hell," he said, "I was just praying he didn't
count the money I gave him. It's one reason I wanted
to leave so quickly."

"Huh." I really couldn't think of anything else to
say. Other than the three hundred and ten for Crazy
Climber, we had nothing. This could certainly pose a
problem for us.

Then, he said something that surprised me. "I'm
sorry, Jay. That was the dumbest thing I've ever done.
I got swept up in the moment. I guess I figured I could
get some of your lost money back. It just happened so
fast, y'know?"

No matter how mad, disappointed or depressed this situation made me, I truly couldn't blame my friend for his decision or for the contest itself. Having known this guy forever, I have seen him play Galaga countless times. In all the time we'd played against each other, I had been the victor maybe three times, to somewhere in the ballpark of a million second-place showings, and I knew my way around that game like nobody's business. Practically no one could beat me, except for Austin Ridenour, of course. Quite simply, he was the best Galaga player I knew. A heavy sigh snuck past my lips. "I know, dude. But in all honesty, given the same situation, I would've bet on you too. The guy looked like an inbred redwood. Who knew he could play?" But it didn't change our dire situation one iota. Now, we faced a serious dilemma. "Question is, should we continue onward to Weedpatch, or tuck our tail between our legs and scamper on home?"

"We're so close. Let's get there, get Crazy, then we'll figure out something. Maybe we can get some money from your parents."

The thought of begging for money, especially from my folks, made me bristle. I lay in the lumpy bed for a while, worrying myself to sleep.

When we left the next morning, our gas gauge sat just above the empty line, and we really had no clue what to do about it. Racking our brains, we had the brilliant idea of collecting a bunch of beer cans and bottles from the sides of the road and returning them to a grocery store. However, we quickly came to the realization we were not in Michigan anymore. No state between Texas and California had a bottle return policy.

We had to do something drastic. Locating a used music store, we sold all of the CDs we brought along on our journey. Though Austin had the majority of the discs we sold, I lost a few of my favorites as well.

Unfortunately, the cranky old guy at Capital Records & CDs didn't think our selections had very much resale value. Thus, we only received thirty-five dollars for the ten CDs.

As we ambled back to the truck, we couldn't help feeling sorry for ourselves. "What a sad day for our intrepid heroes," Austin said quietly. Though I thought I saw a tear in the corner of his eye, I chose to refrain from comment.

However, at least it got us a full tank of gas and a small amount of non-nutritional food-like substance. So, with full and slightly queasy bellies, we continued our journey to Weedpatch.

We drove in relative silence through New Mexico, listening to the static on the radio. Every now and again, if I fiddled with the knob enough, the static became a song. As the last half of *Layla* dematerialized into a hissing crackle, I finally gave up and clicked the thing off. Approaching a sign informing us of an upcoming town named Moriarty, Austin pointed at it. "Say, isn't Moriarty Bonnie's last name?"

A sigh escaped from somewhere deep inside. "Yeah, sure is. I wonder how she's doing?"

Turning momentarily to glance at me, he asked, "So how you doin'? You okay?"

Shrugging, I replied, "Eh. Sure, I guess." I paused for a moment before continuing. "Y'know, come to think of it, I actually am okay. It just occurred to me that I'm not as devastated as I should be. Why do you suppose that is?"

"Did you love her?"

I stared at him for a moment. I honestly can't recall him ever using that word in the context of a woman. He had used it to describe all-meat pizzas and Galaga, but never a woman. "Love... Man, I don't know. We would've been together a year in July. Or was it August? Something like that. Anyway, there were times I liked her more than others. I probably loved her. I mean, I said the words all the time. But I don't know. Right now, honestly, I feel more relief than sadness. She bitched a lot. Didn't seem like anything I did pleased her. She didn't like my friends."

"Your friends didn't like her, either."

After saying that, Austin had the biggest smirk on his face, so I chuckled softly. "Yeah, I gathered that. She especially despised you, for some reason."

"Oh, I know why. I'm one of your few single friends. I think she thought I'd corrupt you, like I'm some sort of playboy. In reality, she should've adored me. Instead of going to bars or strip clubs, we'd sit around watching wrestling or playing games on your Atari Jaguar."

"Yeah, except she really hated video games, too. Most women do, I guess, but she loathed them with a passion. I never could understand exactly why."

"For one, she sucked at 'em. And two, she probably felt she was competing against them for your attention. And she didn't win very often. So she lost playing them and she lost trying to keep you from playing them. Lose-lose. And here you are, driving to the other side of the country because of another game. It's no wonder she chose this moment to dump you."

I had to marvel at Austin's grasp of the human psyche. Suddenly, I felt a strong urge to ask a question. "Why is it that we've never talked about your divorce?"

After a small pause, he ran a hand through his thinning hair. "You never asked."

"Didn't I? We've been best friends forever. I really didn't ask? Are you sure?"

"Oh, you knew I didn't want to talk about it. You could tell, so you didn't ask and I didn't say. It worked for both of us. We play video games, eat fattening food and drink rum and Cokes. That's the kind of friends we are. And that's cool." He turned and smiled. Though it looked forced to me, I decided not to call him on it. Not often do friends define their friendship. Neither of us had much touchy-feely in our genetic makeup. In this exchange, we had talked more about our feelings than we had in the previous decade. It had to be enough.

He turned back to the road, and I switched the radio on once again. "Oh look, the static song. I love this song." I started singing, or actually hissing, some invented tune. Austin joined in, and we laughed our way across New Mexico.

Other than piss stops, we drove non-stop all the way through Arizona, eventually finding ourselves in Weedpatch, California. As would be our luck, we pulled into the driveway of the current owner of our Crazy Climber machine in the wee hours of the morning. To add to our mounting bad luck, the rain came crashing down to the ground like a faucet cranked wide open. Though I told him I'd sleep in the back, clearly that plan wouldn't work. Two in a cab would be a tight, uncomfortable fit, but I guess it worked out okay. Honestly, I didn't actually remember falling asleep, or even having pulled into the guy's driveway, for that matter.

I awoke to the sound of rapping on the driver's side window. Prying my bleary eyes open, I caught sight of a tall, lanky man staring in at us. His face harbored a look of annoyance and amusement, not an easy combination to display. When I glanced over at Austin, I understood the guy's amusement. At some point during our snooze, Austin's head had dropped onto my shoulder and he managed to deposit a decent sized amount of drool onto my shirt. I gave him a gentle shove away from me as I rolled down the window. "Uh, hi," I stammered, still foggy from my slumber, "I'll take a number two with an orange juice and coffee."

"Anna Coke," Austin mumbled, without opening his eyes.

"Uh, yeah," the tall, casually dressed man replied. "Are you Jay?"

That woke me up enough to get with the program. "Oh, yeah. You're Bill, right?"

He smiled as he nodded. "Why don't you boys come inside. I'll get you that coffee, and we can get you Crazy Climbing."

Austin finally popped his eyes open as he fumbled for the door handle. "Already feels like we've been crazy climbing."

We both got out of the vehicle, and began stretching vehemently. I thought my body popped and cracked a lot until I heard Austin's. Several of his joints popped in rapid succession, reminiscent of gunfire. Bill looked at us sympathetically. "It couldn't have been easy sleeping in that confined space." He opened the door to his house as he continued. "Ya know, you could've knocked. I have a spare bedroom."

As we entered his large, modestly equipped domicile, I shook my head. "At three in the morning? Nah, don't think so. To be honest, we weren't positive we had the right house. It was raining pretty hard."

"Oh, it rained? I must've slept through it."

I heard Austin mutter something under his breath, so I quickly said, "Nice place. So, where do you keep the game?"

"Downstairs." He handed me a steaming cup of coffee and pointed toward a box of doughnuts. "Help yourself to some breakfast. They're day-old, but still pretty good."

Frankly, they tasted more like two-day-old doughnuts, but it really didn't matter. Compared to the way things had been going, this tasted like paradise with cherry filling.

Trudging down the stairs and into his game room, I let loose with an impressed whistle. He had a couple other classic games down there, like Defender and our beloved Galaga, and had another already crated and ready for shipment. "All these machines are sold. I got a really good price for Defender, nearly triple what you boys paid for yours. And there she is," he said, stating the obvious as he gestured toward the game that had already captured our attention. It looked good, minus the scratches on the outside of the cabinet. As we both stared at the 'attract mode,' watching the machine play itself, he handed Austin the key to the coin holder. "It's set to play for quarters right now, but you can change that with the dipswitch settings. I've got the manual over here."

At that point, it occurred to me that I had neglected to bring the money in from the truck. I excused myself as I galloped up the stairs, making a quick detour to grab a couple more of those stale little pastries first. After stuffing them in the glove box, I rummaged around in my bag until I found the wad of cash stashed in the bottom. Yanking it out, I began thumbing through the bills as I ambled up to the front door.

Reaching for the door handle, my heart dropped like the Climber in the game after being hit in the head by a flowerpot. My initial count only came up with three hundred and five dollars! I recounted it, but still came up five dollars short. I had no idea how; we never touched this money. But when I scrutinized the five, I realized what might have happened. It was one of those stupid new bills! They looked so similar to each other. I have heard countless horror stories of cashiers giving out change for a hundred instead of a fifty, and so on. I must have seen the five and mistook it for a ten. Hell, I didn't even know the new fives had come out yet.

I had my hopes the guy would understand our plight. After all, he seemed like a nice, laid-back fellow. Perhaps once he heard our tale, he would cut us some slack. After all, it was only five bucks.

As soon as I mentioned the money situation, his brow furrowed and his face became a stern facade. "Look, this machine already sold for a lot less than I expected it would. I was hoping for at least double that amount, but that's what you get when you sell stuff in an auction."

While explaining our dire situation to Bill, I watched over his shoulder as Austin casually opened up the coin box. When I caught the glint of a pile of quarters, Austin turned to look at me. A huge, evil grin crept upon his face. He bent down and quickly started pocketing the coins as I did what I could to keep Bill's attention away from my devious little friend.

After he cleaned out the change box and stuffed it in his pocket, he quickly locked it again and sidled up to me. "Oh dude," he said as he thrust his hand in his pocket, "don't ya remember? I borrowed that fiver from you to get quarters, so I could play Galaga in the arcade we passed near Atlanta. It should all be here."

He pulled out the handful of quarters and counted out five bucks, handing them to Bill one dollar at a time. At that point, Bill said, "Oh, say, that reminds me. I think there's still a few bucks of mine in that coin box. Here, give me the key."

Austin successfully hid his smile as he dropped the key in Bill's outstretched hand. When the guy kneeled down, opened the box and saw no coinage, he uttered, "Huh. I coulda sworn there was..." Then, he looked up at my friend and probably saw something untoward in his eyes, or perhaps caught the slightest upturn of his lips. Recognition sank in, and the look became a fiery glare. He opened his mouth as if to say something, but decided against it. Standing up, he tossed the key at Austin before turning his attention to me. "Fine. Get your game and leave. I have a lot of work to do today."

It wasn't easy lifting that heavy arcade game up those steps, Bill staring daggers at us all the while. I found it oddly humorous, paying him with his own money, and seeing how mad losing five bucks had made him. However, all that humor didn't help us get the thing upstairs, and by the time we reached Ol' Red, my back ached something fierce.

After loading it in the pickup and securing it against the back window with bungee cords and a bright blue tarp, we hit the road to head back home. However, things couldn't have been any bleaker. After paying for Crazy, Austin still had a dollar fifty from the coin box. Even though not particularly funny, we both felt the need to laugh heartily over that one. Not like a buck-and-a-half, a quarter tank of gas and couple of hardening fat cakes would get us anywhere near home, but still, we had to laugh, to keep from crying.

We drove up US15 as far as that tiny amount of gas would take us. This propelled us to a town called Littlefield, Arizona, just across the Nevada border. In the late afternoon, we pulled into the parking lot of a small convenience store called Mom and Pop's Soup to Nuts. It had a cozy looking restaurant attached to it, complete with red-and-white checkerboard drapes adorning the windows. With all other options exhausted, we knew we had to call someone and get some money wired to us. We ambled over to the pay phone and gave it a shot.

My first call went to my parents, who didn't answer. "Oh well, I doubt they could've figured out how to wire the money anyway."

Austin phoned his folks next, who refused to accept the collect call. "No," he screamed at the operator, "not Boston. Austin! Tell them it's Austin, their son. No, I...Hello? Crap!" He turned back to me and shook his head. "Who in their right mind would name a kid Boston? Sheesh!"

From there, we took turns calling our siblings. My brother Ben had his money tied up in the stock market, while Austin's sister Sandy was trying to scrape up enough funds to fix her busted dryer. I couldn't even find a working phone number for my sister Elsie.

"Well," Austin said as we sat with our feet dangling off the bed of the truck, "I'm running low on options. What about you?"

"I have a couple cousins I haven't spoken to in years. That'll be a fun sell."

As we continued listing off and shooting down possible loan candidates, a young boy approached us. At a little under five feet tall, I guessed his age at around twelve. He had ruler straight, short brown hair and a friendly demeanor. With his eyes glued on the machine looming behind us, he pointed and shouted, "Hey, what's that?"

This stopped our chatter as we gazed down at the boy. After a moment, I replied, "It's probably before your time, kid. It's an arcade game called Crazy Climber. Ever heard of it?"

When he shook his head, I stood up on the truck bed and removed the tarp as I gave him a brief rundown. "You've got this dude, see? He's trying to climb up the building, using the windows for hand holds. But the windows are opening and closing. If a window closes on his hands, he falls. Also, you've got little old ladies tossing flower pots at ya, King Kong trying to smack ya, and birds flying by, pooping on your head."

The boy giggled at the poop comment. "What's with the two joysticks?"

"Ah," Austin proclaimed, "that's the beauty of it. The one stick controls his left hand, the other for his right."

"No fire buttons?"

"Nope. You can't hurt anything on the screen. All you do is climb up, moving from side to side to avoid things." I moved my hands in a climbing motion.

"It's simplicity at its finest," added Austin. "You against the building."

"Sounds cool. Can I play?"

Austin shot the kid a large grin. "You got a quarter and an extension cord?"

I tried really hard not to laugh out loud, but I pretty much failed. When he turned and ran away, I momentarily felt bad, but not long enough to stop snickering. "Okay, so where were we? I can't ask my Aunt Betty for any money, not after last Thanksgiving's fiasco. How about your..."

However, the young man surprised us when a minute later, he came running back with a quarter in one hand, and the female end of an extension cord in the other. My smile faded. "Um, kid..."

My buddy dropped a hand on my shoulder, whispering, "Hey man, a quarter's a quarter."

The boy handed the cord to Austin, and he went around back to plug it in while I helped the youngster onto the truck. As I lifted him up, I asked, "Are you sure this is okay, using that store's power?"

He smiled and tossed a thumb toward an older gentleman who had just emerged from the store. "My pop owns the place."

"Well, then. Cool! Have at it."

While he began playing, I hopped down and marched over to Pop, hand outstretched. If anyone had the look to be called Pop, it would be this man, with his grayish-white hair, a face full of deeply grooved wrinkles and an affable smile. Shaking my hand with a firm grip, I introduced myself. "Your boy called you Pop. What should Austin and I call you?"

He continued his infectious smile. "Oh, everybody in these parts calls me Pop. I see no reason why you shouldn't do the same. Thank you for letting James play your game."

"Actually, Pop, I should be the one thanking you. We're kinda stranded here until we can get a family member to wire us some cash. Even though it's only a quarter, it'll help."

"At least we can buy a Coke now," added Austin as he approached.

"Down on your luck, boys?"

"Yes, sir." I fidgeted around nervously as I continued. "We started out with plenty of money, but a robbery and, well, other circumstances have drained our resources." I informed Pop of our situation while his boy played our game.

"My goodness, that's rough."

"Sure is, sir. We're just now trying to figure out our next move."

When James yelled, "Aw!" in the background and turned to look at us, I knew he'd already lost the last of his lives.

"What'd ya think, James?"

"It's fun! Can I play again?" Before I could answer, a boy with dull red hair and freckles sauntered up. James looked down at him with a huge, toothy grin. "Hey Sam, check this game out! It's pretty cool."

Pop dug into his pocket and handed James several more quarters. "Here ya go, boys. Enjoy." Then he turned back to us. "If ya don't mind, that is."

"Not at all," I replied with a genuine smile. "We bought it to play, after all."

We ended up staying there until nightfall. Not only did James like the game, but as the afternoon dragged on, other neighborhood kids began lining up behind our truck with quarters in hand. Even Pop hopped up and took a turn, although he couldn't get the hang of it and tumbled off the first building repeatedly until he hit the ground, covered in bird poop. Still, I believe he enjoyed himself. "Well, I always liked pinball better," he uttered with a pathetic grin.

As the sun set and the neighborhood boys scurried off home, an adorable older woman pushed open the door, leaned out and bellowed, "Dinner's ready, Pop." The stout woman's hair glistened as white as freshly fallen snow. I didn't have to ask if this was Mom, but a moment later, Pop confirmed it.

"Thank ya kindly, Mom. Did ya make enough for everyone?" He turned and winked at me.

"Of course, dear. The more the merrier!"

"Come on in, boys. She always makes too much." When Austin and I exchanged nervous glances, he added, "What we don't eat today becomes some sort of Goulash or Casserole Surprise tomorrow. You'll be doing the neighborhood a favor, let me tell you."

I looked at Austin and shrugged. "Okay, sure. Thanks!"

"Not a problem." Pop led us in to the diner. "So fellas, where's home?"

"Lansing, Michigan."

"Oh glory be," Mom shouted from the kitchen, "I used to know some people in Michigan. Do you know Bob and Carol Navarre?"

Austin and I exchanged comical glances. Why do people always assume you would know someone just because you're from the same state? "Um, no ma'am."

"It's too bad. They're good people."

As we sat down at a large, round table with a checkerboard tablecloth matching the curtains, Pop said, "You sure traveled a spell just for a video game."

Austin answered before I could. "It's not just a video game to us, sir."

"It's how we met. Austin and I have been friends for nearly twenty years now, but when we first started talking, it was anything but social. Oh sure, we had seen each other around DeWitt Middle School, but we didn't talk until High School, around 1981. We both wasted our afternoons at the local pizza parlor... What was that place called again? Buddy's? Buffy's?"

Austin shot me the queerest look. "Dude, it was Terranova's. Downtown."

"Right," I chuckled, "Terranova's. I was close." I continued before he could say anything. "They had a room with a dozen or so video games."

"They had a few classics from that era," added Austin, "like Frogger, Pac Man and Scramble. I was wicked bad at Scramble."

"I was just bad. Anyway, I was playing the old Space Invaders game, getting my butt handed to me."

"And I was playing Galaga, which had come out earlier that year. I wasn't very good yet, but I sure enjoyed giving it my quarters."

"Then, the owners wheeled in this new machine. Crazy Climber." The memory gave me a nostalgic smile. "They sat it in the corner and plugged it in."

"As luck would have it, we both lost the last lives on our respective games at the same time. Without noticing each other, we congregated over to this new machine."

"It seemed like it had some mystical, quarter-sucking power," I said, becoming momentarily aware of how bizarre and nerdy this story sounded. "We stood nearly shoulder-to-shoulder, staring at it. Then, we both whipped out our quarters and tried to insert them at the same time."

"We bumped, both our coins jostled from our hands. Mine landed a few feet away, but Jay's rolled behind the machine."

"We've been over this, dude," I said with mock anger, "your quarter rolled away. That was mine lying there."

"No it wasn't."

"Yes it was!"

Austin looked over at the family and noticed they were growing a bit nervous, so he let out a laugh. "Anyway, we actually came to blows over it."

I shrugged. "We were geeks, what can I say?"

"Which means it wasn't much of a fight. But either way, the owners kicked both of us out for a week. We whined, we did the whole 'he started it, no he started it' argument, but they didn't care."

"We stared through the glass as some punk eighth grader not only came in and started playing Crazy Climber, but he picked up both of our quarters to do it!"

"Yeah, it was pathetic. But it eventually led to our friendship. So, weird as it sounds, I think we both look at Crazy Climber as the game that began our lifelong connection."

I nodded in agreement. "And as the months rolled on, we played that game quite a bit. It definitely became a favorite of ours."

We got so carried away with the telling of the story that neither of us paid much attention to the rather lavish meal we found ourselves in the middle of eating. When it occurred to me, I paused in mid-bite. Mom saw this and grew concerned. She asked, "What's wrong, dear?"

"Oh, uh, I…this meal is fantastic, but we only have the few quarters we earned on the machine today. We can stay tomorrow and earn the rest of what we owe you, if that's okay with you."

Pop waved a dismissive hand our way. "Oh, you fellas don't need to worry. The meal's on the house."

"But, you can certainly stay tomorrow if you wish," added Mom as she gave us a slice of some truly delicious apple pie. "Now, Pop told me a bit about how you got here, but the price for your dinner is to share the tale with me as well. Pop's memory ain't what it used to be."

We again told the story of how we arrived at this fine establishment.

After we completed the tale, Mom stood over us, wiping the table with a small square of red-and-white checkerboard cloth. "It's a good thing you boys ended up here."

"Fate," Austin said simply as he popped the last bite of apple pie in his pie-hole.

"You folks have really saved us," I said, "and we both appreciate it. Now, if you don't mind us asking, what's your story? How did you become Mom and Pop?"

Pop's real name was Will Myers, and he'd been in Littlefield all his life. "Never saw much point in going elsewhere, to be honest."

"You used to speak fondly of Phoenix," added Mom, who introduced herself as Missy. "But then along came James." She tossed a wink toward her young son.

Pop waggled his fork at her. "Oh now Ma, ya know I was never goin' anywhere. This store's been in the family for three generations now. My daddy, Pop number two, built the restaurant side. We're simple folk, in a simple town, and I'd have it no other way."

"That's beautiful," Austin said.

"Indeed." I turned to Austin as a yawn slipped out of me. "Well, I don't know about you buddy, but I'm whipped. So, do you wanna sleep in the back with the game, or in the cab?" Not like I expected him to volunteer to sleep on the hard steel of the truck's bed, but I wanted to give him the choice.

However, before he could answer, Mom spoke up. "Oh, I think not! We have a spare room. You are both sleeping there tonight, and that's that."

"Wow, that's very sweet of you, Missy."

"It's nothing at all," she replied as she wagged her finger at me. "As long as you call me Mom."

Once we tossed our tarp over the top of Crazy, we went inside. We had the best night's sleep since leaving Lansing.

In the morning, we got up and popped open the coin box. Surprisingly, we ended up netting around six bucks. Though certainly not enough to get us very far, it did give us an idea of how we might be able to make it home under our own power.

We stayed in Littlefield for the day, and being a Sunday, we had quite a turnout. According to Pop, we had every kid from miles around lining up to try to get that little man up the building. I felt like a carnival barker, standing on top of the cab of Ol' Red, yelling, "Step right up, boys and girls, big and small! Come up and try your luck. Can you get the Crazy Climber up the building? Help Crazy survive the perils. Come aboard the Crazy Truck, and..."

From the ground, Austin interrupted me. "Crazy Truck?"

"I'm thinkin' on my feet here. What, ya like Crazy Mobile better?"

"I like 'shut up' better, honestly."

"What?! Someone needs to draw the kids in," I said incredulously.

Austin waved his arm in a wide arc. "Dude, every kid in town's already here. Who ya barkin' to?"

My buddy had a point, of course, but I hardly cared. I found myself having a good time, yelling for all the children to hear. We even had several adults tossing quarters in our machine. Some of them remembered playing this game in their youth, while others felt the need to satisfy their curiosity.

One guy, a thick man with a goatee and a glaringly shiny bald head, hopped up into the bed of our truck. He held his quarter proudly as he proclaimed, "Step aside, mortals. I, Ernie Castrol, am the best player ever. I will put my high score atop this beast."

I assumed Austin had the same thought as me... freak! But no, not my game-playing brother. He looked over at the man and pointed at him. "So, ya think yer all that, huh?"

"And a bag o' chips," he replied, causing the kids to cackle loudly.

"I challenge thee, oh shiny-headed one, to a ten-dollar bet. What say ye?"

Panic flushed through my body, realizing my friend could lose a decent chunk of what we had just earned. "Dude," I whispered with a bit of a nudge to his solar plexus. "What are you doing?"

He shot me a quick glance. "Dude, we're not gonna get home unless we take some chances. I got this covered. Besides, this isn't Galaga."

I winced at the memory, but I sighed and stepped back. Austin waved the man up to the machine, again uttering, "What say ye, friend?"

Ernie smiled and nodded while producing a ten from the pocket of his torn jeans. "Ye says ye's in... uh...heck, forget the Medieval speak. You're on."

Austin let the big man play first. He played fairly well, but barely made it to the third building, whereas my man Austin topped that building and one more after that. I always marveled at his game-playing acumen on this game, especially in comparison to me. Though a pretty decent player in my day, I never did see the third building myself. I kept getting nailed by those falling barbells and steel girders at the start of the second building.

At the end of the day, our success flabbergasted me. Amazingly, we had nearly thirty bucks to our name. It seemed impossible until I did the math. "Okay, I counted sixteen kids and thirteen adults. If each one played twice, and a few played three times, that still doesn't do it. Well, that one kid played several times. Oh right, and the ten-dollar bet. Wow, I guess so." After showing the heap of quarters to Austin, we both did a happy dance.

"This'll get us a full tank, with money to spare." It still wouldn't see us home, but today's proceedings filled us with confidence.

We got an early start the next morning, preparing to hit the road at first light. Pop saw us packing up our meager belongings and moseyed over to us. "You sure ya gotta leave us now? Mom will be disappointed."

I walked up to him and stuck my hand out. "We need to head for home. Thank you again, Will, for everything."

Returning my handshake with a firm grip of his own, he gave me a refreshingly honest smile. "You're welcome, son. Remember, you'll always be welcome at Mom & Pop's. Hope to see you again sometime."

As Austin took his turn shaking Pop's hand, Mom came out from the store. Practically bounding, she held a large wicker basket in her hand, her trademark checkerboard cloth covering it. "Oh dear, I almost missed you!" Moving amazingly fast for her age, she ran up and placed the basket delicately in my hand. I smiled warmly and darn it, I swear I nearly popped a tear. They were being so lovely to us. I really didn't want to leave.

Lifting the cloth, I inhaled the aroma of a nice pile of chocolate chip cookies, sweet rolls and a couple of tiny pies that appeared to be blueberry. I spun, handing the basket to Austin. When I turned back, Mom had me in a bear hug. Okay, I admit it. That tear squeezed out from the corner of my right eye, and it brought a couple friends along with it. Overwhelmed by their generosity, I squeaked. "Thank you, Missy."

She shot me a look only a mother can give, so I whispered, "I mean Mom."

# SEVEN

We drove up US15 until it intersected with US70. At this point, we tossed the rest of our money into fuel and convenience store burritos, or in other words, gas and gas. Heading east, we drove until both tanks, the truck's and our stomachs, contained only fumes. This got us around the Salina, Utah area.

Deciding our best bet would be to stick to the smaller towns whenever possible, we drove past a road sign with the name Gooseberry on it. Austin pointed and chortled. "Sounds like a real down-home type of town to me. I wonder if we can get us a hunk of gooseberry pie."

"Haven't you had enough pie?"

Looking at me like I just insulted his manhood, he replied, "Dude, c'mon. There's no such thing as too much pie."

I shook my head slowly. "Okay, fella. Well, regardless, we're not gonna make it much farther. I have no idea how long Ol' Red can sit on empty before she's truly empty."

"Say, isn't Utah one of them Mormon states?"

I shrugged. "That'd be all we need, a place without electricity and us looking for a place to plug in."

Austin chuckled. "No dude, that's the Amish. I'm more concerned about the possible lack of alcohol."

"Ah." When Ol' Red coughed and we felt her lurch, I sighed. "We haven't got a choice. She's starting her death throes."

At around three o'clock in the afternoon, we rolled into Gooseberry. As we came upon the parking lot of a small bar called Fuller's Place, experiencing either karma or car empty, our red Chevy S-10 sputtered and stalled. We exchanged worried glances, realizing our fate rested with this place. "Well," I said, "it is a bar, so I guess that answers the alcohol question."

We both knew how much of a challenge it would be to get the truck started again. Running a vehicle out of gas, which we had both done in our lives, always caused a bit of a hassle. I did it when I was seventeen, on my way to St Johns. Ironically, Austin rode shotgun on that trip as well. I still remember the embarrassment we felt, walking door to door, begging for gas. After knocking on several doors, and having those doors slammed in our faces, we managed to find a friendly old guy who not only took us into town to get more gas, but also lent us his gas can. Still, it took over a half an hour to get that old baby blue Mustang of mine started again. Being that young and so naïve, I actually thought I had killed the thing.

Austin and I hopped out of the truck and walked up to the plain, wooden building. As we approached the front door, I noticed the square, wood grain structure had no windows. It gave me the impression of being one of those hardcore bars, for people serious about their drinking. Apparently, sunlight was no friend to the professional drinker.

With my confidence faltering a bit, I grabbed at the heavy, wooden door and yanked on the large handle. It only moved about a half an inch before hitting the deadbolt with a loud, echoing thump. Apparently, the place hadn't opened yet, although I saw no sign alluding to its hours of operation.

As I turned to Austin and opened my mouth to speak, the door suddenly swung open, nearly smacking me in the side. I leapt out of the way like a rabbit from a hound-dog, then turned to see this gigantic tree-trunk of a man staring down at us. This dude had to be at least a foot taller than we were, and easily weighed a hundred pounds more than my miniscule, borderline anorexic frame. I figured this guy could bench-press both of us and still have a hand free. "Hey," he bellowed, "We're closed! Come back at four."

Shaking off my momentary trepidation as he pulled the door shut, I shouted, "Wait!" When he did, I quickly continued, "Um, we're in a bit of trouble here. Wondering if you could help."

He stared down at us, his hand still wrapped tightly around the door handle. "I'm listening."

"Well, see, we're driving cross country with that arcade game," I tossed my thumb over my shoulder, toward the truck, "and we were robbed of our money. Our gas tank is quite literally empty, and we have no way home unless you help us."

A nasty scowl enveloped Mister Tree-Trunk's rugged face. "I'm not giving you boys any money."

"No no, sir, we're not looking for a handout. All we ask is that you let us hook up that arcade game in your parking lot and collect the quarters."

Austin added, "Yeah, if we're lucky, we'll earn enough to get us some gas and a meal, to make it to the next town."

"One night only." Still looking up at him, I forced my best smile.

He continued to stare down at us for what seemed like an eternity. I doubted he cared one bit for our plight, and I can't say I blamed him. This man had his own place to run, after all. But finally, his façade softened. "Tell ya what? I'll do ya one better. You can bring that thing in the building. We'll set 'er up in the corner and charge fifty cents a play. I keep half."

We both simultaneously said, "Cool! Thanks!"

Fuller's Place was nothing but a clean, simple watering hole, to be sure. The interior had a large, wraparound counter with the obligatory bar stools, a few tables and booths spread about, dart boards, pool tables and one lone arcade game. Galaga, of course, sat in the far corner. When our gaze fell upon it, our hearts dropped. This once proud game had really been punished. The monitor and cabinet had scratches and initials carved all over it, the front looked sticky with beer and Lord knows what else, and very little joy remained in the joystick, since it had developed a permanent lean to the left. I gave the stick a waggle and it felt loose and sloppy. It reminded me of a prizefighter after the big bout. We brought Crazy inside the small, dank bar and hooked it up next to the dilapidated Galaga.

"Nice place ya got here," I said to the big guy, who eventually introduced himself as the owner, Gus Fuller.

"No it's not, but it keeps me goin'."

As I spent some time chatting with Gus, Austin stood next to me, his gaze fixed on Galaga. He just couldn't turn away, sporting a look reminiscent of that old TV commercial with the crying Indian staring at a pile of garbage. Apparently, he couldn't take it anymore. "Hey Gus, ya mind if I do a little work on this thing?"

"Naw, knock yourself out. The tools and stuff are in the back. I'll get 'em for ya."

The next hour rolled by with Austy giving Galaga a good working over while I sat on a cracked vinyl barstool, telling Gus about our journey thus far. When I got to the part about having my money stolen, Gus's eyes narrowed to slits. "So what did ya do to the skank?"

"What could I do? She bolted, and we had to leave early the next morning."

He shook his head slowly. "Ya can't let people walk all over ya like that. Did ya go to the cops, at least?"

"We tried, but the cop shop was packed. We just didn't have time. We had to roll." I didn't enjoy lying to Gus, but this line of questioning bothered me. Like I needed anyone else firing up my anger or further provoking my embarrassment.

"I'll tell ya, if it was me, I woulda stayed there, searched every inch of that city until I found her. One way or another, I would've gotten payment outta her. No one steals from Gus Fuller. So ya say she got cash and your Visa card?"

"Yeah." That sent up a red flare in my mind. "Oh geez, I still have to cancel that stupid thing. Could I possibly use your phone? Oh, and a phone book?"

Reaching under the counter, Gus brought both items up for me, plopping them on the counter. I sat there for a few minutes, wracking my brain. Giving me a puzzled stare, Gus asked, "What's wrong?"

"My credit card company has changed names and banks at least three times since I got it. It used to be Prodividend, then became USA Bank, and then...what...City something. Gah, I've lost track." I panned through the business section of the phone book for a while. I found a City Card company, but when I called them, they said they couldn't help me unless I knew the credit card number. The irony was completely lost on the guy. "I lost the card. How am I supposed to know what the card number is?"

"Why sir, simply check your last statement."

"I can't. I'm on vacation."

"Well, good for you! Enjoy your vacation and call us when you get home."

"No, but you don't understand..." Too late, the guy hung up on me. "Crap."

Gus came back into the room. "Any luck?"

"No. I got transferred three times, then got hung up on by a moron named John with a thick Indonesian accent. Ah well, I'll have to deal with it later. Never mind this. Tell me about life in Gooseberry."

"Not much to tell. It's not so bad here, but it gets kinda boring. That's why the locals come here to get drunk, beat the crap outta the place and each other. Somethin' to do."

That did not comfort me much. "Um, say there Gus, is our pride and joy gonna be safe here tonight?"

His mischievous smile did not help to quell my fears, but still, his reply of, "If anyone abuses your video game, I'll abuse them," eased my mind a little bit.

Just then, Austin came bounding up to us, gesturing toward the machine with pride gleaming in his eyes. "Come, take a look!" The three of us walked over to inspect his handiwork. "There! Whatdya think?"

My buddy did quite a job on it, all things considered. Not only had he removed the layer of sticky filth, but he also tightened up the stick and even managed, somehow, to buff out many of the scratches on the screen.

"That's amazing, kid! I don't think it ever looked that good." He gave Austin a heavy slap on the back. "Grab a beer and sit back. The show's about to start."

"Yeah," I said to my buddy, "Gus's been telling me how wild this place can get. But he promised to protect ol' Crazy."

"Besides," Gus added, "today's a Monday. It shouldn't be too rowdy here."

Gus Fuller was correct. We didn't witness our first barroom brawl until nearly ten o'clock, apparently a couple of hours later than usual. Having led sheltered lives, this turned out to be quite fascinating, watching human nature in action directly in front of us. Okay, I'll stop talking like a nature show host watching a pack of cheetahs ripping apart a gazelle from the safety of a cheetah-proof bubble. Frankly, we both felt pretty freaked out by the evening's turn of events.

We sat at a small, square table Gus had positioned a few feet away from our arcade game. I fashioned a crude sign using cardboard and a marker that read, *Fifty Cents - One Day Only*, and affixed it to the top of Crazy.

Throughout the evening, the machine garnered moderate business. It seemed the later it got and the drunker the patrons became, the more they wanted to play. But unfortunately for us, some of them started growing more vicious.

One guy, who had obviously never even heard of the game let alone played it, challenged another guy's high score. Not much of a score, since he hadn't even made it halfway up the first building, but he stood there with arms akimbo and a smug grin upon his bearded face. However, the challenger, who had an entire beer riding on it, couldn't even survive the 'bird poop' section, the second obstacle in the game, so he lost the wager. This fired him up to a rematch, which we only minded because when he lost, he slammed the left joystick down hard, then kicked the machine. I looked over at Gus, but he had his attention elsewhere, so Austin and I watched the rematch with some trepidation.

Initially, we were overjoyed when the other guy won this round. But the loser got angry and tossed his mostly empty beer bottle at the winner. The drunken fool ducked, but the bottom edge of the bottle caught the top of his head. It caromed and spun on a high arc, spitting droplets of beer across our machine. Luckily for us and for Crazy, the impact of the bottle off the guy's head actually saved the machine, otherwise the bottle would've crashed into the monitor.

But, this started a nice little fight that resulted in four shattered bottles, two busted chairs, several pool cues snapped in half and one demolished table. As for the participants, I counted six men unconscious, one guy with a damaged hand and another with a broken, bloody nose. They bounced off our machine a couple of times, and brave Austin actually leapt in-between some brawlers and the game once, so they bounced off him instead of Crazy. When one of the men witnessed this, he pulled back his arm to punch Austin, but luckily for us, Gus stepped in at that moment and ended the skirmish by breaking a pool cue over the guy's head. Austin breathed with a relieved sigh. "Thank you, Gus."

"No problem. I always keep an extra supply of pool sticks around, for just such an emergency." Gus's wide grin confirmed how much he enjoyed doing that. "Did ya hear that sound? Man, there's nothing like the crack of a pool cue off some guy's fat head. It's just not a great day unless I get to bust a few skulls."

The rest of the night proved to be equally as challenging and entertaining, and I went through a few beers as I watched the festivities. We witnessed the typical type of behavior expected in any given beer-soaked situation, like kicks, punches, slaps and more broken furniture. At least now I understood why Gus chose such flimsy, crappy looking tables and chairs, and charged a cover. Another fight broke out, but since it happened on the other side of the bar, it didn't directly affect us.

Many people played Crazy, and a few tried to abuse the machine in one way or another. I caught one guy pulling out a small pocketknife, to presumably start carving initials in my baby. So I got up, staggered my intoxicated self over to him, and politely told him to stop his foolishness. Well, he chose to turn the knife on me!

Fortunately, being very drunk himself, I easily sidestepped his weak swipe with the tiny blade. At that point, instead of being scared like I really should've been, it pissed me off. So I reared back and kicked him square in the family jewels. Then, when he dropped the blade and fell to his knees, I rammed my left knee into his face. Flopping around on the floor like a mackerel without a water supply, he cradled his manhood with one hand and his gushing nose with the other.

This gave me such a feeling of power and manliness that I scoured the joint, grabbed the first woman I saw, a skinny brunette in a jean skirt, and kissed her solidly on the lips. She took a quick look at my smirky face and slapped me, then shoved me onto the floor.

At this point, both Gus and Austin came to lift me up, each grabbing an arm. "No more beer for you, kid," shouted Gus, as they seated me back in my chair. I smiled knowingly.

During the evening, Austin and I had a rather interesting conversation with a couple of chatty locals. Ben, a thin man with squinty eyes and a mound of coal-black hair scattered across his head, had fears about the coming new year. "Y2K, man," he drawled after taking a swig of his Budweiser. "At midnight on January first, 2000, everything's gonna stop working, man!"

"Yeah," his homely woman Arlene added. "The banks'll lose our money, the gas pumps'll shut off and the nuclear power plants'll blow up!" She shifted her rather sizeable weight and I definitely heard a sharp creak from her wooden chair.

"We're all gonna die man, so we're spending all our money now, before it's too late."

I chuckled as I took a sip of the coffee that Gus insisted I start drinking. Being a computer nerd, I'd had plenty of experience with computers, and I highly doubted anything horrific would happen. But Austin, he had a different opinion, and didn't have a problem sharing it. "Y'know," he said as he polished off a rum and Coke, "there's gonna be some good coming outta this situation."

"Like what?" Arlene asked, while she twirled her back-length brown hair around her index finger.

Austin gave them a sly smile. "Well, all the computers will be erased, so all credit information will disappear." Neither of them seemed too interested in that, so he continued, "as will everyone's criminal and driving records. No more points! The government won't be able to track anyone, either."

Not only did their eyes light up at that, but it also caught the attention of a few guys sitting at the bar.

"Ya think?"

"Fer real?"

"Dude," piped up a tall white man wearing a shirt that read, *Don't Trust Whitey*, "that would be awesome! Maybe I'll go steal somethin' tonight!" The irony of his shirt wasn't lost on me, but clearly so on him.

Feeling compelled to add something to that comment, I said, "Well, no one knows for sure what'll happen, so I wouldn't rack up any new points. One thing is for certain, though. We'll know what's what in about six months."

"I don't know about any of you," said a pungent old man with a whiskered, leathery face, "but I ain't taking no chances. I got me fity gallons of water and enough canned food and ammo to last me 'till aught-one. I'm crawlin' in ma cellar on New Year's Eve and locking maself in."

I hoisted my coffee cup high. "I'll drink to that!"

Randy D Pearson

EIGHT

Late the next morning, nearly noon in fact, we counted our blessings as well as our winnings. Fortunately, Crazy survived the evening with no lasting damage. However, even though people packed the place, we didn't do quite as well as we did the previous day. The coin box had around thirty-six dollars in it, which made us happy until we realized half of that went to Gus. We also feared he would expect us to pay our bar tab out of the winnings. Between the two of us, we most likely drank more than we earned.

Austin and I sat across from each other at the table closest to Crazy, with the change piled up between us as Gus strolled over and clasped his meaty hand on my shoulder. "So guys, how'd we do?"

I shrugged, which felt kinda weird with the weight of his heavy paw on my shoulder. "We raked in thirty-six fifty, so your cut is eighteen and a quarter." I began divvying up the pile of quarters.

He raised his hand off my shoulder, only to drop it back down again as he spoke. "Ya know what, why don'tcha keep it all." Smiling large, he gestured toward the Galaga machine. "Austin here saved me all sorts of money fixing up that game of mine. I was lucky to get a buck a night outta that beast the way it was, but hell, last night..." He paused as he walked over to it and unlocked the coin box. A waterfall of quarters rained out. "Look at that, will ya? That easily pays your cut as well as your rather sizable bar tab."

Gus shared his best grin with us, and it turned out to be infectious. "I'm glad someone was keeping track of what we were drinking," Austin snickered, "cuz I surely didn't have a clue."

We thanked the affable bar owner one final time, packed up our stuff and hit the road a little after one o'clock. Actually, it took longer than it should have. In all the excitement, we forgot we ran the old Chevy's gas tank dry. When it did not start initially, we both freaked. With my hangover, I doubt it would have ever occurred to me. Good thing Austin reminded me of how we coasted in on fumes. So, we had to beg one more favor from Gus, needing a ride into town to fill up a small gas can. Actually, two favors, since we also had to borrow a small gas can from him. Oh well, so much for planning ahead. Even after priming the beast, it still took about fifteen minutes to get Ol' Red to crank over, and when it did, we hustled over to the gas station and topped off the tank.

Once we merged onto the expressway, we drove Interstate 70 up to Denver, then hopped onto 76.

Traffic had been fairly sparse for the past hour, with a few small cars, a station wagon and a couple of semis to break up the monotony of the smooth road. As we zipped past one of the many green signs announcing upcoming cities, the mention of a town called Crook forced me to break out a horrible Richard Nixon impression. "I am not a resident of Crook."

Austin rolled his eyes at me, saying nothing as his attention returned to the passenger side window.

"Okay, fine. Let's talk about celebrities."

"Do we have to?"

"Come on, you'll enjoy this, Austin." So, I manned the wheel and we chatted mindlessly about which celebrity female we'd most like to bang. As I made the case for Cameron Diaz, citing *There's Something About Mary* as my primary argument, a semi up ahead of us blew a tire. The truck, one of those massive fifty-three footers, swerved gracefully as the tire shredded, tossing pieces of jagged rubber into the air directly in the path of several cars, including us. We hit a smaller chunk with our right front tire, momentarily launching us off the pavement. Crazy took a small vertical leap, but fortunately, the bungee cords held firm. However, the sound of the machine slamming back onto the truck bed caused me to cringe.

A couple other vehicles didn't fare as well. An old-school wood panel Vista Cruiser station wagon hit a large piece of rubber head-on. The driver, clearly not equipped to handle such a circumstance, spun the wheel hard and skidded sideways. The large wagon caught the side of the road and left the ground, rolling over a couple of times before landing on its wheels, hitting the grass and sliding to a stop. Another car, a poop-brown Celebrity, also took a bit of rubber to the grill, but the driver worked through it with no additional trouble. After that, we had to deal with a lot of screeching tires and swerving cars.

While I wasn't normally the sort who bothered to help in situations like these, something compelled me to pull off the road and stop. It may have been Bonnie's lingering voice in my head, telling me how I never think of others. Perhaps I was doing this to prove her wrong, but I'd rather think of it as my good deed for the year.

Either way, I had barely stopped Ol' Red when I flung my door open and bolted over to the wagon, with Austin in hot pursuit. The seat-belted driver appeared to be unconscious, with her head tilted at an uncomfortable angle and her hair splayed across her face. My arrival at her door coincided with that of another driver, a tall, annoyingly handsome man with tightly cropped black hair and unnaturally white teeth. The two of us worked in an unspoken tandem. I grabbed the handle and yanked the heavy Vista door open as he reached in, unlocked the seatbelt and pulled her out.

After gently setting the still-unconscious woman on the ground, he looked up at me. "Is anyone else in the vehicle?"

I walked over and took a peek inside. "No, just her."

At that moment, she opened her eyes, took one look at the man kneeling over her and showed him a weak smile. "You saved my life," she said softly.

He smiled back, and told her not to move. I decided to take that cue to head back to the truck. Austin jabbed me with his elbow. "You should go over there and take some credit."

Hopping back in the truck, I replied, "That's not why I did it. Let pretty-boy over there be the hero.

Besides, if he hurt her by yanking her out of the car, something you're not supposed to do mind you, let her sue him, not me."

"Spoken like a true hero."

"Shut up."

Easing back onto the road, we drove the rest of the day without incident. We continued on I-76, then jumped onto 80, since it seemed a marginally more direct route home.

When it got to be around ten o'clock and we had just passed the Colorado/Nebraska border, we opted to stop for the night. We had, once again, dumped the last of our money into the gas tank, so we thought it prudent to find a cost-free way to sleep tonight. The secluded campground in the small Nebraska town of Ogallala seemed a perfect destination for us, so we pulled in and found a nice spot in the back. Austin took the cab, as I opted to sleep under the stars. Wandering a ways away from the truck, I found myself a nice patch of grass and fell fast asleep in the warm Nebraska night.

A drop of water brought me back to the land of the conscious, hitting me in the face just below my left eye. I popped my peepers open to witness a very dark and gloomy morning indeed. The clouds hung thick and heavy, signaling an imminent downpour. Propping myself up, I gazed over at the truck.

I almost passed out at what I saw, or rather didn't see. Springing to my feet, I sprinted over to the truck, yanked the driver's side door open and yelled in at the still-sleeping Austin. Not surprisingly, my friend didn't budge, snoring a snore that certainly would have drowned out the horn, had I succumbed to the urge to lean on it. "Austin!" I screamed as I shook his body frantically. "Wake up, numb nuts!"

"Uhhh," he grunted as the sleep slowly dissipated from his mind. "Wha? Brekfas?"

"No, not breakfast," I said slowly. "Take a look out the back window, okay?"

"Kay." He yawned and stretched as he turned his head. "Oh. Uh, where's Crazy?"

"A-Ha!" I shouted right at his face, inadvertently spraying spittle droplets all over him. "That's the question, isn't it, Sleepin' Ugly? Where, indeed!"

Finally, recognition seeped into his brain. "Holy crap! How?"

"Yeah, that's another good question! Someone dragged the machine off the truck while you snored away. Hell, it could've been a pack of wild bears, with that mating call emanating from your noise hole all night."

He hopped out of the truck and we both jogged back to the empty truck bed. Staring pathetically at the back of the truck, we noticed they didn't steal the blue tarp, at least.

At this point the rain, which had been merely an occasional drop heretofore, began falling a bit more steadily. It wouldn't be long, I suspected, before it became a full-fledged monsoon. "Okay, where could it be? It can't have gone far. And wherever it is, it is probably getting rained on. We..."

Austin held a hand up and I paused mid-speech, stopping just in time to hear a faint, "Awwww!" permeate the rainy air. We listened intently, and as he pointed toward the campground's pavilion, I thought I heard some electronic beeps amidst the sound of the rain patting off the ground. Grabbing the tarp, I tried to keep up as Austin bolted toward the commotion.

As we approached the pavilion, we were somewhat relieved to see several teenagers huddled around

Crazy, cheering the player's progress. Though upset, I couldn't help but be amazed this campground had a pavilion with electricity. I didn't camp out much, so maybe this sort of thing happened all the time, but it seemed curious to me.

A couple of the teens turned to see us standing there, dripping wet, and alerted the others. The only one who didn't look our way was the kid at the controls, and I really couldn't blame him. After all, he had already scaled most of the third building. That certainly wasn't an easy task.

"Having fun with our machine?" Austin growled, trying to look all tough and angry by folding his arms and scowling. I attempted to add my own menacing demeanor to the ambiance, but I couldn't find a masculine way to fold my arms while clutching a large, blue tarp.

The boy at the controls spoke without looking away from the game. "Man, dude, you guys sure are heavy sleepers!" That impressed me. Not only did he manage to climb his way to the top of the third building, and hold a conversation while doing so, but he used *man, dude* and *guy* in the same sentence.

"Yeah," one of the others said, "we tried to wake you, but dude, it just wasn't gonna happen."

"We, uh, we didn't want your game to get rained on." This came from a little guy in the back. "So, y'know, we did you a favor."

"Ya gave us a heart attack," I muttered, "if ya call that a favor."

The player began scaling the fourth building, but lost a life right away. During the death screen, he turned to look at me. "Sorry, dude, but when you're camping in a park and it starts raining, it can get real boring real fast."

"Then," added a redhead with bad acne, "we heard what we thought was a bear in heat, so we came to investigate."

I gave Austin an evil glare, but he stood there chuckling along with these kids, so I dropped my hostility.

We hung around in the pavilion until early afternoon, at which time the rain tapered and eventually ceased. We managed to pull in another few bucks, plus Austin won a bet with the player kid for a ten-spot. The kid, once again, made it to the fourth building, but my buddy smoked him by getting to the same spot without losing a life. Oh Austin, such a good little climber!

During our stay, we got to know those kids pretty well. They all went to school at Ogallala High, ranging from Brian, the fifteen-year-old acne-ridden redhead, to Darrell, the eighteen-year-old we first saw playing. Max, the smallest of the bunch with a bowl haircut, pointed a bony finger toward their campsite. "We're gonna get the fire blazin', dudes. Ya wanna sit with us?"

"Yeah," added Brian, "we got hot dogs and marshmallows. You're welcome to join us."

As Austin and I exchanged glances, I realized we hadn't eaten today. "Well, we are hungry. I mean, if ya don't mind."

Darrell turned from his friends to give us a wicked grin. "If, maybe, you men could do us a favor in return?"

Oddly enough, my mind flashed to *Deliverance* and I involuntarily shivered. Austin, ever the smarter of us when it came to innuendo, flashed a return grin. "Sure, if you got the money. You boys got a favorite beer?"

All six of them named a different beer in unison. "I heard whatever's cheapest. I'm on it."

While Austin did the beer run, I stayed behind, instead choosing to give my arcade machine the once-over. So far, it had weathered the journey fairly well. It had a couple of smudge marks at the base, undoubtedly where a few pairs of work boots had either brushed up against it or had kicked it. There were some sticky dots here and there, probably beer or pop spillage. I licked my thumb and rubbed them off one by one. Plenty of fingerprints also adorned the screen. Since I didn't have any Windex, I did the next best thing, using the eyeglass approach. Breathing heavily on the screen, I got it good and foggy, then used my shirt to buff it clean. The teenagers looked at me funny, but refrained from commenting.

As I read the instructions printed on the cabinet, I realized something for the first time. The main character didn't have a name. The game simply referred to the dude in the green jumpsuit as The Crazy Climber. How odd and unimaginative. I pointed it out to the teens, and asked, "So if you had to name The Crazy Climber, what would you call him?"

They shouted out all sorts of goofy names, such as Doofus Magnus, Rufus Magillaculli, Rufus Doofus, which I kinda liked, and Roger. Brian looked at Darrell and crinkled his brow. "Why Roger?"

"Don't ya think he looks like Roger McCaffrey, from fifth period science? Lookit the hair!"

They all chortled, but of course I didn't know the kid, so I smiled politely and turned back to the game.

As I continued staring at it, it occurred to me that thus far, I hadn't actually played Crazy Climber. I'd driven Crazy, I'd cleaned Crazy and I'd protected Crazy. But I hadn't played a single game yet. After going to all this trouble, driving all these miles and running all these schemes, I hadn't felt the warm embrace of the machine on which I had spent my hard-earned money. So, I opened the coin box, popped out two shiny quarters and relocked it, pocketing the key. Sliding the coins into the machine, I began to play.

I always appreciated the simplicity of Crazy Climber with its two joysticks, one to control each hand. No other game consisting of two sticks, but no fire buttons, came to mind. The sticks still had a very tight and responsive feel, which made me smile all the more. Like most video games from this era, once I found a groove, once in the rhythm, the game played like a dream. Left stick up/right stick down, then switch positions quickly and up a row of windows I went.

Fighting the first building hard, I lost a life when a bird trapped me on the edge and pooped on me. Not long after, I lost a second life by taking a flowerpot to the head. I actually survived one pot shot to the skull, which up until now I didn't realize was possible. Apparently, if the green-jumpsuited one had both hands securely gripped on the windowsills, instead of falling, he'd make this hilarious, "Uh" noise when it bounced off his noggin. But after that, I ran past all hazards, even managed to time the big ape near the top of the first building, and made it to the roof. I waited for the helicopter and it eventually came, whisking me off building number one.

However, I barely saw the second building. The first barrage of steel girders and iron dumbbells did me in, just like in the old days. Anger momentarily bubbled up inside of me, but it rapidly faded when a realization hit me. I now owned this machine. Once I arrived home and got this baby secured in my basement, I could play over and over until I got it right. Eventually, I would conquer the second building, then the third and the fourth. Oh, the fun I'll have!

Austin returned fairly soon after my game ended, and the eight of us sat by a now-roaring fire, drinking cans of Lodestone beer and laughing. After discussing the details of our journey thus far, we delved into deeper subjects. It cracked me up, listening to these young punks discussing their allegedly trouble-filled lives. Derrick, for instance, had girl problems. He emptied a beer down his gullet and sighed. "Dude, I've been with Monica for, like, ever and ever! Like, two whole years! But dude, she's been looking at this dickweed in fourth period, and she all like wants him and even though she says she doesn't, I can tell she like totally does."

"Does what?" I got lost.

"Want him."

"Ah. Well," I replied, "the best advice I can give you is, don't be jealous. Or at least, don't show your jealousy."

"It's the fastest way to push a woman into the arms of another," added Austin.

Max's loud belch reverberated off the neighboring trees. "That's deep, man."

"Hardly. But for certain, it's a better lesson to hear than it is to live through. Trust me on that one."

"So," Tim, who had been fairly quiet up until now, asked, "what about you two? You married?"

"Or just living together in sin?" Brian smirked as everyone erupted in laughter.

Austin and I exchanged longing stares, but we both busted up giggling. "Eh, chicks don't really dig us," I said with a shrug.

"Speak for yourself, dude! I beat off the ladies with a stick."

"It's not the only thing you..."

Austin held up a finger and shouted, "Ah! Now now. There are children present."

The teens started pelting us with pebbles and twigs, and we all enjoyed a laugh. "Actually, my woman just left me, right before we started this journey. And Austin here got divorced a couple years back, on the grounds of physical cruelty." Their horrified facades lit up the night air, so I clarified. "He beat her off with a stick. What'd ya think?"

After the laughter subsided, Derrick grabbed a fresh beer and waggled a finger at both of us. "So, what, do neither of you have jobs? How can you get all this time off?"

"I quit my job," Austin replied. "It sucked. I was just a drone, surrounded by stupid people."

I hadn't thought much about the real world, and it came flooding back at that moment. "Crap! I'm on a one-week vacation from my office job with an insurance company. What day is it, anyway?"

"Wednesday." Since the fire had died down a bit, I couldn't see who answered me.

"Well, I'm officially three days AWOL. I'll have to find a phone in the morning and try to smooth things over."

"But for now," Austin said with a large, stretchy yawn, "it's late and I'm pretty buzzed. I'm crashin'. Later, gentlemen."

We both said our goodbyes to the kiddies and ambled off toward our truck. This time, I snoozed in the cab while my esteemed colleague passed out on a patch of grass a little bit too near Ol' Red. If I thought Austin had a deafeningly loud snore normally, his noise-making skills increased by a factor of three when drunk. Even through the closed door, it rang loud and clear. Fortunately, I had consumed enough beer to make nodding off a quick and effortless task.

In the morning, the boys helped us get Crazy back in the rear of Ol' Red. "Again," the redhead said, "sorry about scaring you guys like that."

"Eh," I replied with a shrug, "no harm, no foul. Thanks for not letting Crazy get dumped on." With that, we hit the road again.

We only had enough money for one tank of gas, and that didn't even propel us to Lincoln, Nebraska. We decided to check out the road signs and allow the town names to guide us. Though I thought McCool Junction had a great vibe to it, when Austin saw Beaver Crossing, well, he had the wheel, and away we went.

The *Welcome to Beaver Crossing* sign listed the population at a mere 548 people. It seemed to have the necessities, like a grocery store, gas station, church and a bar. Of course, we set our sights on the bar. We took bets as to the name the bar would have, in a town named Beaver Crossing. Austin thought Trim Tavern would fit nicely, but I opted for the more mundane Beaver Crossing Bar. When we came upon the building with the name BC's Place plastered on it, I decided I won. Not that I actually won anything, but still, victory for me.

Unfortunately, the word dump did not do this place justice. In fact, calling it a dump was an offense to all dumps everywhere. As we entered, the smell of stale beer, pee and desperation permeated our nostrils with a vengeance. I can't say I looked at all forward to having Crazy stuck in this place.

Well, as it turned out, we had no need to fear that happenstance. The bar owner, Brian Cooper, or BC to his friends (which meant I didn't actually win the bet) wasn't at all keen on helping two young fellows down on their luck. Even though we looked disheveled due to sleeping in our clothes, and probably smelled a bit funky as well, BC had no interest in helping out us, "fancy city folk," as he sternly referred to us. Without any fanfare he showed us the door, practically by the scruffs of our necks.

"Well, crap," I said to the sky. I turned to Austin and shrugged. "We have no money, no gas and no bar. I guess this is the end." A large, exaggerated sigh escaped from somewhere deep within my soul.

Austin sat on the back of the pickup, his feet dangling off the edge. As he spoke, his voice carried a sinister-sounding undertone. "Well then Jay, we really have no choice, do we?" Before I could ask him what he meant, he held up an index finger before hopping up and walking across the street to the grocery store. I started to follow, but he spun around and held up that same finger again. I assumed he wanted me to stay put, so I took his seat on the bed of Ol' Red.

After a few minutes, he came sprinting out of the store with something bulky tucked under his shirt. I again sighed heavily. Great, now we've resorted to common thievery. As my buddy came running up, he whipped out a wad of extension cable from inside his jacket. "Don't worry bud," he assured me, "We'll give it back as soon as we're done."

"Done doing what?"

Continuing with his wicked grin, he hopped up on the truck to plug in the female end of the cord to Crazy, then leapt off the side of the Chevy S-10 with the male end in hand. Sneaking over to the back wall of BC's, he bent over and plugged it in. Nervously, I uncovered the game system, removed the bungee cords and opened for business.

It was a weird night, to be sure. Standing on the bed of the pickup, we waved to people as they entered or exited the bar, suggesting they hop up and give Crazy a whirl. Also, we flagged down cars as they sped by.

Though we had a pretty decent business going, we knew BC would inevitably catch on to our activities. When he found out, he and four of his biggest patrons came over to have a chat with us about the concept of stealing customers and electricity. I jumped off the truck and marched up to him, hoping I could assuage his hostility. "I know how this looks BC, but really, we're not stealing your customers. We..."

Oh, he wanted nothing to do with my explanation. The fact we disobeyed his orders clearly aggravated him more than anything else we did. Things quickly escalated from bad to worse when one of the guys extracted a wooden baseball bat from under his long leather duster, hopping up on the bed of our truck. When he raised the bat over his head directly in front of Crazy, I screamed like a little girl watching a horror movie.

At that moment, our truck roared to life, so I turned and made a dash. One of the thugs grabbed the collar of my shirt, but I yanked my neck forward, ripping the shirt a bit. Then, I kicked back with my right leg, impacting meat of some sort. That got him to relinquish the hold, and I ran with all my might. The sudden forward jerk of the truck made Bat Boy wobble and topple off the truck bed and down to the ground. Austin pulled ahead only a few feet, enough to dump the guy off and stun him, which allowed me precious seconds to dive in the back of the truck. Then he floored it, tossing gravel all over the unruly mob.

I landed heavily upon my stomach, just in front of Crazy, then spun around on my belly to locate our adversaries. As I glanced back, horror filled me when I noticed my arcade machine rapidly falling toward me! Quickly, I rolled onto my back and put both hands up, bracing for impact. When the machine hit my hands, I quickly remembered how much this stupid thing weighed. Basically, I didn't stop the machine's forward momentum as such, but ended up using my body as a softening mechanism. In other words, the damn thing fell on me! As it slammed into my hands, both wrists popped simultaneously, then both elbows followed suit.

So there I lay, sprawled out on the bed of the pickup, underneath a large video game unit. While Austin continued to accelerate, old Crazy went crazy on me, bouncing up and down on my body. As he seemingly hit every stupid pothole on that bumpy old road, it felt like I was being dry-humped by a refrigerator.

Finally, after a couple of minutes that seemed like an eternity, Austin pulled off the road to check on me. Jumping out of the cab, he dashed to the back, but once he saw my predicament, he couldn't help chuckling. "Dude, that's certainly a unique new way to play the game."

A witty retort did not immediately come to mind, so I just politely asked him to, "Get this damn thing off me, already!"

After a cursory examination of Crazy, we couldn't find any obvious damage. My bony body lessened the blow considerably.

However, both my wrists felt like I had just stopped a runaway train. Since I could still move them, I assumed I had no broken bones or anything, but I definitely pulled something. Or pushed something. Either way, they both ached, and I only saw one real problem with that. Until I healed up enough, I wouldn't be able to help move the machine at our next destination. We decided in the future, no matter what, we would leave the bungee cords attached. That way, if we ever had to vacate another location in a hurry, Crazy would be securely fastened to Ol' Red.

Though we didn't do all that well in BC's parking lot, we managed to pull in enough coinage to splash some gas into Ol' Red's tank and allow ourselves a couple of candy bars.

Our next stop would be, by our estimation, two jumps away from home. We figured we had enough gas to get us somewhere near Des Moines, Iowa, then off to Chicago, then home. So, for now, we needed a small Iowa town to plug in at. This time, I informed Austin I would choose the city, since his last choice left something to be desired. Pleasant Hill, I surmised, sounded like a lovely, game-playing community.

We pulled into town in the late afternoon, nearing the apex of a beautiful, sunny day. After driving around for a few minutes, wondering how long the gas vapors would last us, we found a nice, little party store called Jenkinson's, on the south side of the city. We met the owners, an affable-looking husband and wife team who looked to be in their mid-fifties. After explaining our dire situation and flashing them our best puppy-dog eyed, pouty-lipped, sad-faced expressions, they looked at each other, turned back to us and flatly refused to help. "Ya look like filthy hippies to us," the woman said.

"You bums need to get jobs," the husband added. "Hit the bricks!"

As we ambled back to the truck, Austin glanced over at me and couldn't help but laugh, despite our situation. "Nice choice, ya filthy hippie."

"Yeah, yeah. Geez, I did *not* see that one coming. They seemed so nice."

"Not pleasant at all. It's apparently not a criteria for living here."

"See, and I figured we'd find a sign here stating, 'You have to be this pleasant to enter our town.' Boy, was I wrong."

"Clearly. But it does explain why you've never visited Hell, Michigan."

"Hell, yes," I responded. "Sounds far too hot and pitch-forky."

Austin put his open hand under his neck. "You must be this evil to enter our town."

Laughing as we climbed into the truck, we peered down the road as far as we could see. "Say," Austin said with a point of his index finger, "does that look like a bar to you?"

"Ya mean the one with the Sunset Tavern sign? Nah, I doubt that's a bar. Most likely a church."

Giving me a glare, he slammed the truck in gear. "You better pray they help us. I don't see much else on this street that would work."

Rolling on down the street, Austin turned in to the Sunset Tavern's parking lot as Ol' Red coughed.

Exchanging nervous glances, I leaned over and gazed at the gas gauge. "We're beyond empty again. Crap."

From the outside, the Sunset Tavern appeared to be a decent sized establishment, with an outdoor patio overlooking a lush, overgrown area on the back end of the parking lot. Inhaling deeply, we dislodged ourselves from Ol' Red and sauntered inside.

Pushing open the door, we immediately regretted being thought of as filthy hippies at the last place. Although the inside of this bar looked pristine and well maintained, with a smattering of patrons enjoying meals and booze, we could hear a high-volume shouting match going on somewhere beyond our vantage point.

We stood in place for a couple of minutes, listening to the profanity-laced tirade, before a tall, red-faced man stormed past us and pushed his way out the door. An even taller woman with an even redder face chased after him. Shoving the door wide open, she screamed, "Keep walking, moron! Don't you ever come back here!" The angry woman stood close to six feet tall, with pale, smooth skin and midnight black hair hanging down to the tops of her eyes, her bangs ruler-straight.

Coming to a halt directly in front of us, she looked down and forced out a sharp exhale of air. "What kinda idiot comes in a half-hour before his shift to quit? A stupid, ungrateful idiot, that's who. If I weren't a lady, I'd rip his throat out and feed it to the stray dogs. Christ!" She paused momentarily, took a deep breath, then said in a marginally quieter voice, "Sorry about that. I hate stupid people. I can't help it. Now, do you two want food, or are you just here to drink?"

This certainly wasn't the best introduction we could've hoped for. I rather wanted to sprint out of there at top speed. However, I knew we had few alternatives. "Well, as much as it pains me to admit this, I think we fall into the category of stupid people. We're trying to make our way home to Michigan, but we have no money. We have an arcade game in our truck that we've been setting up at bars and restaurants, relying on the meager amount of quarters to get us to the next town."

While I spoke, she gritted her teeth tightly. I could see her jaw muscles tighten through her cheeks. When I paused, she replied, "Oh, and you expect me to let you put this thing in my bar, I take it?"

Austin jumped in with, "Did we mention the stupid people bit yet? We hate being dumb, but it's beyond our control."

As she stood scowling down at us with arms akimbo, I didn't much like our chances. Though not fair to judge someone on a first impression, she seemed to me to be an abnormally angry woman. Shaking her head slowly, she said, "You know, I'm not exactly inclined to help you guys, but here's the deal. The moron I just kicked out of here was my waiter for tonight. I have other employees of course, but I doubt I can pull anyone else in on such short notice. This place will get busy later on, and I'll need the help. So, if you two work as waiters tonight, I'll let you put that game of yours over in the corner and you can keep all the money it earns."

Austin and I exchanged nervous glances. I had never waited tables before, and Austin's only experience, if you could call it that, was his three-week stint at the old Burger Jack fast food joint. Being up against the wall, we knew we had little choice. "Okay," I said to her, "it's a deal. How much does it pay?"

Wow, did that question make her laugh. She actually had to wipe tears from her eyes before she replied. "Oh, I'm not paying you. If you want to put some dumb video game in here, that's the condition. Otherwise, hit the road and I wish you luck in finding another place to help you. There's only one other bar around here, and it's a biker bar on Elmwood. Good luck with that one."

Though her self-satisfied smirk really irritated me, all three of us knew she had us over the proverbial barrel. Clearly, it was either her way or the biker bar. Besides, we couldn't be sure Ol' Red had enough petrol left in her to even get us there. Again, I looked over at Austin. We then stared up at her and nodded.

She graciously gave us about an hour before our shift started, so we went outside to get Crazy ready for the show. Even though my wrists still ached, she fortunately had a dolly we could borrow to wheel it inside.

After a couple of minutes, I heard a discouraging "Uh oh," fall from Austin's mouth. In our haste to vacate the last town, we hadn't unplugged Crazy from BC's electrical outlet. Though the extension cord did unplug from Crazy, it almost yanked the power cord right off the machine. He had to remove the cabinet so he could get to the wiring. Waiting anxiously, I stood by like an expectant father from the 50s, smoking in the waiting room while awaiting news of my newborn.

Unfortunately, it did yank on some of the internal wiring, and there would be no way to know the extent of the damage without running some diagnostics. Obviously, we didn't have the tools available to do that. We were looking at the real possibility of having to rewire the entire power system, which would take a day at the earliest, under the best of conditions. If we had to do it now, well, we would quite simply be screwed.

Using the tools available, we made the best of it. "The handyman's secret weapon," proclaimed Austin as he held up a roll of silver duct tape. He also located some electrical tape to bandage the stretched power cord, and after fastening the cord to the cabinet with a generous amount of duct tape, we held our breaths and powered her up.

Success! We had to be careful not to let the cord stretch at all, or else the game would flicker or cut out completely for a second. Having that occur would be enough to lose all progress and cause the machine to reboot. Once we got it securely packed against the far wall, we started her up and placed our slightly wrinkled *One Day Only* sign up top.

After completing that task, we reported for duty. Standing in front of her, she stood like a Drill Sargent inspecting her troops. Pointing a narrow, manicured finger at me, she said, "You don't look too bad, but you definitely need to shower and shave. I have a uniform that'll fit you. But you," she pivoted and jabbed the same finger at Austin, "I don't want you in front of the customers, fat boy. They'll lose their appetites. You can wash dishes." With disdain evident on her face, she tossed an apron at my stout friend.

Understandably, he looked hurt and angry. We both wanted to comment on her overt rudeness, but we bit our respective tongues.

Grabbing me by the upper arm, she yanked me forward. "Come. You can get cleaned up in the back." With that fanfare, she led me around the corner and up some stairs. We came upon a small room with a futon, mirror, toilet and sink. "I sleep here sometimes," she said matter-of-factly. "I bring men here when I don't want them in my real bed."

"Okay." I guess that takes lesbian off the list of possibilities. "So, uh, what's your name?"

"Jackie. Now go ahead and get ready. There's a razor in that cabinet."

I pulled my shirt off, and began the cleaning process. As I lathered up, I glanced over at Jackie. She stood there watching me, with a look that could've been either lust or disgust. I really couldn't tell. "How long have you had this bar, Jackie?"

"I inherited it from my father several years ago. I run it with an iron fist and it makes more money than he ever did."

"Yeah, I don't doubt that. You seem to have a handle on things."

"I could do a lot more with better staff. But I've learned to lower my expectations."

"Good to know. With that in mind, you should know I've never waited tables before, but I'm a quick learner, so I might not disappoint."

Shaking her head slowly, she said, "Oh, you'll disappoint. But as long as you don't drop hot food in anyone's lap or cold beer on someone's head, we'll both survive this night and you can go home. You said Michigan?"

I finished washing and began shaving the stubble from my face. "Yes, Lansing. It's the capitol. It's been quite a journey. Ya wanna hear about it?"

"Not particularly, no." Without skipping a beat, she added, "You've got a decent body for a little guy. Good abs. You must work out."

Man, this chick speaks her mind! "Uh, yeah, when I'm home. I haven't been able to do much during the last week or so, but normally I'm pretty up on it. You, uh, you look good too."

She snorted, crossed her arms and turned away. "I know. Don't forget to wash your hair. The sink's big enough, but make sure you wipe up any spilled water when you're done. The uniform's on the bed. Come down when you're done, and don't dawdle."

"Yes Mistress Jackie," I whispered.

Upon completing my sanitation process, I dressed in the supplied uniform and left her man room. Jackie then introduced me to the other two waitresses. "Molly, Betty, this is..." She paused, pointing her open hand my way.

"Oh, I'm Jay. Hi."

After a couple of subdued hellos, Jackie continued. "He's only here today, so there's no need to be very nice to him, or to even bother remembering his name. He's never been a waiter before, so he'll be terrible at it. Help him where you can, but handle your own customers first. And as for you Jay, don't get in anyone's way and for God's sake be careful. Do not make me regret this."

Nodding, I said, "I'll do my best."

"Do better than that."

"Yes, ma'am."

I tried to look at this situation as a learning experience. Not that I wanted or needed to educate myself on the finer points of waiting tables, but I decided I'd try to have as much fun as possible. Knowing my boss had little to no expectations of my competency actually eased my nerves a bit. After all, I couldn't do worse than she already expected me to do, so what the heck, right?

The first valuable lesson I learned was to hold the large, round serving tray with both hands. After watching Betty one-hand it around a tight corner, I figured I should give it a go. I came within a held breath of dumping a plate of nachos, a cheeseburger and two beers all over some fat guy. Fortunately, Molly sprinted by at that moment and using her free hand, she gripped the tray at the last possible moment. With wide eyes and a rapidly beating heart,

I thanked her profusely. "Don't mention it. Seriously, don't. Just use two hands from now on."

This being a tavern, I didn't have to worry too much about food orders. That said, I dished out a fair number of chicken fingers, buffalo wings and other food-type items that didn't actually exist in nature. It led to an interesting conversation with a table of drunken college-age girls. "Whatdya mean?" asked a gorgeous blonde when I told her there was no such thing as chicken fingers. "They're right here on the menu. You guys out of 'em or something?"

"No," I said with a stupid grin, "I'm saying chickens don't have fingers."

"Well, whatdya call those things on the ends of their feet?" She clearly thought she had me with that one.

"Uh, I call them toes. I can get you a basket of chicken toes, but I don't think they'd fill you up. They are crunchy, though."

The blonde didn't find it amusing, but her friends did. They all yelled for me to bring them baskets of chicken toes. Then, all semblance of order broke down. A stunning brunette with pale blue eyes pushed her long hair off her shoulder and demanded, "Bring me turkey lips, buffalo humps and a plate of your finest monkey hooves!"

"Ooo, sorry, fresh outta hooves of any kind. I have monkey wings and monkey knuckles."

When they started chanting, "Monkey knuckles! Monkey knuckles!" I knew I stepped in it. Walking away, I had no idea what to bring these chicks.

I wandered a few feet away from the table before being confronted by Jackie. She smiled, which startled me. "Okay, that was a bit funny, I'll give you that. But you see why silliness has its price? You walked away without getting an order. That does me no good. I'll save you this time, but keep the levity in check."

"Certainly, boss."

Then, she grabbed me by the scruff of the neck like I was a disobedient puppy, parading me back to the table. "Ladies," she said with no expression on her face, "this man doesn't know our menu. You've all been here before, so tell him what you want, slowly and clearly, so he can comprehend it."

Oh my, did those women laugh at my plight! It embarrassed me, but I knew I caused this fiasco, so I grinned and let them order their food. The brunette said, "Bring me the fingers of chickens, and make it snappy."

"Me too. I told you chickens have fingers," added the blonde, clearly pleased with herself.

I smiled at her and nodded. "The customer's always right. I'm on it, ladies."

As we vacated the table, I turned and thanked Jackie. She replied by cuffing me sharply on the back of my head. "Now get to table eight. Their beers are nearly empty."

I spent the next several hours ushering beers, mixed drinks and plates of bar food to a wide variety of clientele. They ranged from sloshed college kids trying to score with one another to a couple of scraggily, white-haired men.

In particular, the old guys amused me to no end. They were sitting at a corner table, drinking Maker's Mark on the rocks while playing game after game of Chess. However, I don't think either of them knew the rules of Chess, as they seemed to be moving any piece to any square seemingly at random. Walking up to them with two fresh Marks in hand, I had to ask, "So fellas, who's winning?"

They looked up at me and grinned through stained teeth. "Today, Glenn is ahead."

After watching Glenn move a knight two squares diagonally, I felt compelled to say, "Um, I don't know a lot about Chess, but I don't think that piece moves diagonally."

The men cackled violently before the one not named Glenn replied, "Oh, this isn't Chess, really. Neither of us have a clue how to play, so we made up our own rules. The horsy can gallop two squares in any direction."

"Actually," Glenn added, "they can all move wherever they want. We just come here to drink and stare at the chickies."

"We call this game Chest. As in, we play so we can stare at their chests. Get it?"

That gave me a good chuckle. "Okay, sure. This way, ya both win. Nice!"

"Damn skippy! Now put the drinks down and get to steppin'. You're blocking the view."

"Sure thing, fellas."

Every now and then, I glanced over at Crazy in the corner. Though relieved I didn't see anyone abusing my beloved, I can't say I saw many people playing it, either. I only noticed a few folks, mostly younger guys, having a go at it. But still, even though I mostly sucked at this whole waiter thing, I had collected a decent amount of tip money. The fact that Jackie had no intention of paying us annoyed me a bit, but once I received my first tip, I realized her game plan and it eased my mind considerably.

The clock chimed midnight before Mistress Jackie allowed me a fifteen-minute break. I headed in the back to see how Austin's dishwashing duties had gone thus far. Hard at work, he gripped a handheld device reminiscent of a small shower-head on a long, coily hose, spraying down a pile of plates.

"Hey Austin, how's the job?" When he turned, I busted up laughing. I can't say what tickled me more, the filthy white apron or the clear plastic hair net. "Oh my God, dude, you look like that lunch lady from middle school!"

Glancing around quickly, he made sure Jackie wasn't watching before he pointed the showerhead thing in my direction, spraying me with a quick burst of hot water. "That's how it's going!"

Backing up involuntarily, I yelled, "Geez dude, watch it! I can't go out there wet."

"And I'm nothing but wet." True enough, he had water literally dripping off his dirty white apron and onto his sneakers.

"Well, at least you don't have to deal with all those drunk idiots, ordering monkey knuckles and moose hooves?"

"What?"

"Well, technically, those were my fault, but still, drunk idiots."

"Still a far sight better than this." He picked up the trash to show me several plate shards. "I've broken two plates so far."

"That sucks. I almost covered a fat dude in food and beer."

"Almost doesn't break the plate. So hey, how's Crazy doing tonight?"

I tossed him one of my patented shrugs. "I've only seen a few people playing, but I've been too busy to pay much attention. But I've gotten a lot of tip money, so we'll be good to go."

"Glad to hear that. I'm not getting' any tips back here."

"I'll give you a tip. Don't break anything else." I had to dodge another water blast. "All right, all right, I'm outta here. But first," I added as I spied a plate with two uneaten chicken strips, "I'm starving."

As I stuffed the chicken in my mouth, Austin looked a bit green. "Dude, gross!"

"I didn't see any bite marks. Besides, I have no idea if she'll even feed us. She's kind of a tyrant."

"And this tyrant is here to tell you your break is over."

I quickly swallowed the bite before turning around. "I know Jackie, I'm on it."

"Good. Hit table three first. And as for you," she continued as she pointed at Austin, "those plates are coming out of the salary I'm not paying you."

"Uh...right. It won't happen again."

"That's correct. This is your last warning." Her eyes narrowed to slits.

The last hours until closing time went fairly smoothly. We had no catastrophes, no spillage, and no more bad food jokes by me or by anyone else.

Once the last patrons vacated the premises at two o'clock, and after a hasty cleanup, she sent Molly and Betty on their way. Walking into the back, I heard her talking to Austin as I entered. "You did a decent job. Only two broken plates, not bad for your first time."

"How did you know I broke those plates, anyway?"

Smirking, she replied, "I know everything that goes on here. You're done for the night. It's going to be a warm night, so you can sleep in the patio area if you want."

Austin looked at me and shrugged his shoulders slightly. "Actually, I'm in the truck tonight. He's the one who'll be sleeping on the patio." He slowly shuffled out the door, and Jackie followed closely behind him.

When the door slammed shut, she turned the deadbolt with a loud click.

I assumed she'd kick me out as well, but instead pointed at the pool table. When I furrowed my brow, she placed her hand on my back and guided, or more accurately pushed me over to it. "Uh, what do you want me to do with this?"

Her response was not a verbal one. She spun me around and shoved me up against the table. Putting a hand on the back of my head, she pulled me in and kissed me ferociously, her tongue like a viper hunting for prey.

Well, I can't say I expected this! Before I could properly react, my shirt hit the table and my pants dropped to the floor.

I must admit, I'd always wanted to do it on a pool table. Not as easy as I'd imagined it to be, especially being several inches shorter than she was, but with a chair and some ingenuity, we managed to find a way.

After a nice romp on the table, pool balls and clothes scattered about, we made our way up to her man room, where we spent the rest of the night. After the rough stuff ceased, she turned out to be surprisingly gentle and giving.

In the morning, I awoke to an empty futon, which for some reason didn't surprise me. Fortunately, she had brought my clothes up and set them on the floor. Dressing quickly, I headed down to the bar.

I found Jackie sitting up at the bar, eating eggs and bacon. Pointing at the kitchen, she said, "There's some in there for you. And if you want to wake your dumpy friend, he can have some as well. I already unlocked the door for him."

"My dumpy friend will wake up on his own." After I trudged in and grabbed a plateful, I sat down next to her. "Last night was great. I really needed that."

Showing me a surprisingly warm smile, she leaned over and kissed me on the cheek. "You weren't bad."

"Neither were you."

"No, I was great. You weren't bad."

"Oh, I see." I couldn't help but grin at that comment.

As I heard the door swing open and Austin came scuffling in, I announced, "Morning Austin. There's breakfast in the kitchen."

"Sweet. I'm famished."

He trudged into the next room, and as I heard him shoveling food onto a plate, I asked Jackie, "So, how'd I do on tips last night?"

"You? You're an apprentice, a trainee. Trainees do not receive tips. Besides, you mostly sucked tonight. You didn't deserve any tips."

Biting my tongue no longer, I yelled, "You took advantage of us all night! You know we were in a desperate situation, hundreds of miles from home, and you've clearly used us for your own gain. It's not right, and you know it."

"Perhaps not, but it's the deal you agreed to. You made some money in that game of yours, and got fed. That should be good enough."

Walking over to Crazy with a loud guttural growl, I pulled out the key and opened the coin box. I sighed loudly at what I saw. "Crap. There's only around eight bucks in here. That barely gets us any gas at all."

I finished up my meal in silence, contemplating how far eight bucks in gas would get us. Looking up, I saw Jackie brandishing a twenty-dollar bill in her hand. "Okay, truth is, you two really helped me out of a pickle last night. No matter how bad you guys were, it would've been ten times worse without you. This is your tip money, minus a few dollars for broken plates."

Leaping to my feet, I gave Jackie a hug, and she returned it with zeal. In my ear, she whispered, "Good luck on your journey, Jay."

Even before the rising sun had vanquished the thick morning fog, Crazy had been packed away and we were on the road once again.

On our way out of town, we passed three other bars and each time, Austin cursed Jackie's name loudly. "Why am I not surprised she lied to us? We probably would've had better luck at any one of 'em. I mean, lookit that one, with all them kids playing in the park right next to it. We would've been so much better off. And I never even saw that biker bar she warned us about. Man, what a liar."

Despite Austin's irate outbursts, I couldn't help but smile. Money can't buy memories, after all.

ELEVEN

We had been on the road for a while now, but with the end in sight, we could finally start to feel a bit relieved. "Oh Austy, we are approaching the home stretch of our journey, and I couldn't be more grateful!"

"You said it, brother."

"Don't call me brother, brother."

"What?"

"Never mind. I know my bed's been calling for me, crying out in the night, and I think my lower back has been answering the call with screams of its own."

Austin shot me a queer look. "Dude, you are so freakin' weird. Has anyone ever told you that you speak like a retarded poet?"

"Oh sure, all the time. It's retarded poet this, and retarded poet that." I rolled my eyes at him. "Sheesh. And you call me weird."

We drove in silence for a couple miles before an odd thought struck me. "Y'know, in retrospect, us losing all our money turned out to be a blessing in disguise."

"Uh, okay, enlighten me, oh retarded poet, but do it in iambic pentameter."

"I have no idea what that means."

"All right then, gimme a haiku."

"Isn't Haiku a Japanese wrestler?"

"What?"

"Yeah, I think he wrestled Shinjuku for the title last year."

"What in the blue hell are you talking about?"

I shook my head. "I guess ya missed that show. He did a pile driver off the top rope. Classic! Anyway, if we hadn't lost our money, we never would've met all those wonderful people and had all these interesting adventures."

"Yeah, but on the other hand, we'd be home right now, well rested and playing Crazy Climber in your basement."

"I know, but look at all that's happened. Would you really trade this for a basement and a good night's sleep?"

"In a heartbeat."

Shaking my head, I replied, "To each his own. The world works in mysterious ways, my friend. If I hadn't been conned out of my money, my life wouldn't have been as spiritually rich. I've spent too much of my life cooped up in game rooms and basements, too much time worrying about my finances. This got me out in the world, experiencing life, meeting people, seeing places I wouldn't have seen otherwise."

Austin clapped his hands together. "Yeah, okay, I get that. But that doesn't count as a haiku."

"Fine. Ya want a haiku. Here: Our cash gone, we have adventures, then go home."

"Bravo. I guess."

"Whatdya mean you guess?"

Shrugging, Austin said, "I really have no idea what a haiku is."

We had hopes of making it all the way to Chicago, but our gas continued to dwindle to dangerous levels. Learning from previous experience not to drain the escape vehicle, we chose to stop in Dayton, Illinois. Dayton, east of LaSalle, was a bit bigger than we had been accustomed to, but we figured it gave us more opportunities to find a parking place for Crazy.

However, initial attempts proved to be less than stellar. We tried the three party stores in the area, and they all said no. Well, one manager told us to screw ourselves, only not using so nice of words. Driving around to all five bars, we got to hear no, or variations of no, from four of them.

The owner of the last bar, a cantankerous man named Frank Wanker, clearly had every intention of turning us down as well. In a fit of desperation, I tried a bit of reverse psychology. "Oh, that's okay, the Longshoreman's owner told us to come back if you turned us down. For some reason, he wanted you to say no before he'd agree. Kinda weird, huh?"

His eyes lit up like someone had set fire to an acre of dry grass. "Oh, Bart did, did he? Oh no, that filthy bastard's not getting over on me this time."

I tried not to smile when I looked over at Austin. After all, it seemed like a really stupid ploy, but it got the guy thinking about his competition, which he clearly hated. So, he reluctantly agreed, as long as he received half of the earnings. "Fine with us."

Frank Wanker, the owner of the Cranky Wanker Bar and Grill, appeared to be one of those guys who spent too much of his life as a bar owner. It probably seemed like a sweet deal to him twenty years ago, figuring he could get drunk every day at his own bar for cheap, while hanging out with all his buddies.

But clearly, the years had taken their toll. He had the look of a sad, angry, tired man, with nearly all of his hair gone except for a small, circular patch of dirty gray encompassing a two-inch ring just above his ears like soap scum on a bathtub. The T-shaped scar on his left cheek looked furious, and his undereye baggage truly resembled tea bags to me. They appeared to be deep enough to smuggle quarters in, with only the tops of Washington's head peeking out. Pennies would be completely lost, I'd bet. Thanks to this man, I finally understood the phrase, *bags under his eyes.*

He told us to move the machine into the back room, but we hesitated. Neither of us liked the look of this bar much, thinking Crazy would be safer in our possession, so we decided not to remove it from the truck.

When we informed Frank of our decision he started to complain, assuming we had every intention of hightailing it before he could collect his money. I thought up an excuse on the spot, one that held some legitimacy. "Hey, we would rather have it in your fine establishment. We'd make more money. But my wrists are shot, so either you and Austin hoist it off, or we leave it." I smiled pleasantly and continued, "It's up to you." Since he walked with a noticeable limp, I figured it was a good gamble.

"Fine," he muttered, "whatever. But hear me good, boys." He moved his face much too close for comfort, accosting us with his stale whisky and cigarette breath. "If you try to screw me over, that machine of yours will be reduced to rubble, and so will you. Ya got me?"

"Uh-huh," I gasped, "Got ya, chief."

The evening started off slowly, but by nearly eleven o'clock, the townsfolk packed the place. This was easily the scariest bar I had ever been in, around or near. I couldn't even recall a scarier TV or movie bar, honestly. Primarily a biker bar, it housed a lot of huge, leather clad men with their huge, leather clad women. Clearly, they did not come to a bar like this to play video games. The way it appeared to me, they came here to fight, drink, play pool and listen to the house band, a hardcore group called The Skunge, while dry-humping each other on the dance floor. However, we managed to get a few of them, and their women, to hop up on the truck and play a game or two.

Unfortunately for us, they all sucked at Crazy and had a hard time dealing with sucking. Those big, mean bastards did everything from kicking the cabinet to slamming the joysticks, and one fat guy belly-bumped the thing, momentarily disturbing the power. In fact, on more than one occasion, Crazy flickered. Then, when this Harley rider's woman had actually made it to the second building, some drunken fool tripped over the extension cord. This totally yanked the plug out from under the case, snapping it off and killing the power. The guy punched the cabinet on the right side, popping a fist-shaped indention into it. Then, he turned to us and sneered. Reaching into my pocket, I quickly produced a wrinkled one-dollar bill. "H...here," I stuttered, smiling pathetically, "refund!"

He stared at me for what seemed like an hour, and after a split second, he snatched the bill from my hand and gave me a hard shove. I tumbled over the side of the truck, landing on the ground with a painful, dusty thump.

Austin, who still stood in the back next to Crazy Climber and crazy man, held up both hands. "Now wait a moment. It was clearly an accident, dude!"

"This," said the gigantic man, "will not be an accident." He then pulled his arm back, his hand clenched tightly in a leather-gloved fist.

When I saw the hairy-scary man's fist, I jumped up, dove into the driver's seat and started Ol' Red's engine. By then, however, I could see in the rearview mirror that he had already taken a swing at my dear friend.

Fortunately, the guy had probably already drank his weight in beer, so I watched through the back window as Austin dodged his first swing. Immediately after his clean miss, he steadied himself and reared back for a really big punch. This seemed like the perfect time to skedaddle, so I slammed it in gear and got us moving. This caught the guy at the apex of his backswing. Coupled with the lurching of the truck and the shove Austin gave him with his foot, this sent the big man tumbling off the back. Through the rearview mirror, I watched intently as the woman gave my friend a most seductive smile before leaping off the back of the truck. She hit the ground on her feet, but we had already generated too much speed for that maneuver to work properly, so she stumbled and fell on her ample butt. This probably angered the locals even more, since they had to assume we heaved her out.

I drove us a couple of miles away before I stopped to check on Austin. Part of me hoped to see *him* lying underneath Crazy, so I could laugh and make a joke as well. But no, of course not, the bungee cords held firm, which was good, of course. Austin looked up at me, exhaustion apparent on his face. "Jay, I don't think I can take much more of this."

I offered my hand to help him up. "I'm with ya there, buddy. Fortunately, it looks as if this adventure is nearly over." We walked toward the cab of the truck, and as we discussed which of us would drive, we heard what sounded like several motorcycles revving from behind us in the distance. Being closest to the driver's seat, I hopped in and got us rolling just as they caught up to us.

By *they*, I meant several patrons of the Cranky Wanker, their choppers screaming in raucous unity. As the biker mob shouted obscenities at us, we feared for our lives. Though we couldn't make out any of the individual hate that spewed from their mouths, it hardly mattered. We knew they were pissed, brandishing bats and chains, wanting to rend the flesh from our bodies.

As quickly as they caught up, the pack suddenly parted, allowing an old, beat-up pickup truck to pull alongside us on the left, its black surface pockmarked with dents and scraped paint. As the truck pulled even with us, the passenger rolled down the window, and we saw Frank Wanker's seething face at the wheel. He shook his fist and screamed, "You boys'll pay for stealin' from me!"

I tried to reason with him. "It's not our fault, Frank! We just..."

But before I could complete my sentence, he plowed his truck into the side of ours. Screaming like a baby without a bottle, I gripped the wheel tightly, doing all I could to keep us on the road. "Ahhh! Okay, now we know where all those dents came from!"

He reared back to bash into us again. Clearly trying to force us off the road, he continued yelling at the top of his lungs. "You'll pay, ya hear me?!"

I really wish I could report our bravery at this point, but in reality, we were both terrified. Other than what happened at Fuller's a few days ago, neither of us had ever been in or even seen a fight. I mean, our little eighth-grade Crazy Climber nerd squabble couldn't hold a candle to this intense scene. Certainly, we had never faced homicidal maniacs with bats and chains, trucks and Harleys. Nothing like this ever happened back home! Having no other recourse, I kept the truck floored, driving as fast as I could with the hopes that they would eventually give up and go away.

The mob, on the other hand, apparently thought if they whipped our truck with bats and chains long enough, and bounced one vehicle off the other long enough, why, we would simply stop and let them beat us to bloody pulps.

No, I did not like that idea one bit. I continued flying down this two-lane road at top speed, my headlights only carving small wedges into the blackness of the night. "Holy crap! I can't see a damned thing!"

"Just keep floorin' it, Jay!"

Like he needed to remind me. Every time one of those leather-clad maniacs swung their weapon at us, the crashing impact made me jump. The hairy guy's chain smacked hard against my side mirror, shattering the glass. The next guy, who had actually donned a Viking helmet complete with horns sticking out the top, roared up on his old-school chopper and beat the mirror right off Ol' Red with one mighty swing of his wooden bat. As it clattered away from us, I screamed, "Oh God, Phil's gonna kill us!"

"Kill you, you mean."

"What? You're arguing semantics?"

"Hey, I'm just saying..."

Our conversation got cut short when another chain crashed against the passenger door.

After several more biker weapon attacks, Wanker again took the lead. At first, he took his mangled black truck and rear ended us. White-knuckling the steering wheel, I fought as hard as I could to keep us on the pavement, swerving and fishtailing wildly but managing to keep us heading forward. He tried that ploy a couple more times, and each time I barely kept it together.

Once he gave up the rear attack, he again crept up beside us, flipped me the bird, and then turned his wheel sharply in our direction. He bounced the Wankermobile into us once again, shoving us off the pavement. Bits of gravel sprayed behind Ol' Red as I fought the pull of the shoulder. The flying gravel showered the bikes behind us, forcing them to pull back.

I managed to angle back onto the concrete just as Wanker pulled up next to again. This time, I decided to take the lead and swerved violently at him. However, Wanker pulled back and I missed him completely, nearly shooting Ol' Red off the other side of the road in the process. As I saw a huge oak tree looming large in our path, I had to ease off the gas and jerk the wheel abruptly to stay on the road. When I heard Crazy bounce in the back, the metal-on-metal scraping noise piercing the night, I inhaled sharply. "Crap!"

When I had to slow down to avoid ramming the tree, it allowed some of the bikers to catch back up, and now we had multiple weapons impacting both sides of the truck. Austin did all he could from his side, tossing everything he could find at the angry mob. Mostly, the food wrappers and soda cups didn't cause much trouble, but he scored a minor victory when he managed to wrap a towel around the face of one of the riders. The Viking swerved sharply, bouncing into one guy before toppling down a ditch. "Yeah! Take that, mutha!"

Unfortunately, our victory was short-lived. Every time one pulled back, another took his place. Oh, the dents! So far, I'd been able to stay ahead enough that none of our windows had shattered. But Wanker simply would not give up, and slammed into us a few more times. Each impact sent the truck skidding off the road, and each time I managed to muscle it back to pavement. My heart felt like it was beating a million times a minute, and I panted rapidly to keep breath in my lungs. "Man, I don't know if I can take much more of this!"

"Hang on, buddy," Austin screamed. Then, he pointed ahead. "Look, a town's coming up!" Sure enough, up ahead I could see the start of overhead streetlights and a twenty-five mile-per-hour street sign. At least I could see the road now, which had to help some.

When I hit the center of town, by that I mean the one stop light, I tried to make a quick left. In that split second, I figured if I could head in a different direction, maybe I could lose them. Or perhaps I'd eventually find the expressway, and maybe a cop would notice us. The Wanker clan would have to give up at that point.

A sound plan, no doubt. However, when I took the left, the speedometer read around sixty. I tried to reduce speed, and maybe made it down to fifty-five, but that hardly mattered. I hit the corner fast enough to momentarily pop us onto two wheels, and that caused my Crazy Climber arcade machine to buck its bungee bindings and leap high into the air.

I swear, what happened next felt like slow motion, like viewing some cheesy movie in a theatre and wondering why I had just spent my money on this crap. My pride and joy, my baby, my Crazy flew through the night sky, silhouetted by the nearly full moon and the orange-tinted streetlight. It hung there like a large, rectangular albatross, slowly rotating past thin, wispy clouds. As it spun, the view screen momentarily caught a streetlight, and from my vantage point, it looked like it had been turned on for a brief, fleeting moment, perhaps saying goodbye to me.

The flight ended, and very quickly. It landed on the cold concrete and exploded with a mighty, cacophonous crash. The impact demolished the cabinet and shattered the monitor, sending glass and particleboard in every direction. The circuit boards and other circuitry flew several feet away and the coin box popped open, showering the ground with an arcing cascade of quarters.

I slammed on the brakes and we both climbed out, staring abjectly at the pieces of my baby. We knew we should keep fleeing, but at this point, neither of us had the gumption. Moments later, the mob arrived, shouting and laughing triumphantly.

Frank walked up and pointed at the carnage, a smugly euphoric grin plastered upon his weather-worn face. "That is what you get for trying to cheat me." Turning to his men, he yelled, "grab my money, boys!"

As the bikers scrounged up the fallen coinage, I shook my head slowly. "I hope you're happy. Go ahead, take the money and leave us alone."

Our eyes locked for a long moment. Though I was certain he could see my sorrow, or perhaps because of it, his joy could barely be contained. He clearly thought about his response before verbalizing it. "No,

I don't think so, punk. We're not done yet. You two still need a beating. It's the principle of the thing."

"Besides," the hairy biker added, "you hurt my Daisy."

"Who, the fat chick?"

My gaze fell to the pavement. "Oh Austin, you really shouldn't have said that."

As they encircled us, preparing to give us an apparently well-deserved thrashing, a police car came whipping around the corner, siren blaring and lights flashing. The hoodlums quickly bolted in all different directions, but instead of giving chase, the cop chose to help us. He slowly rolled over and stopped next to the carnage.

Rolling down his window, he asked sternly, "What happened here, boys?"

"The death of my lifelong dream." My voice barely above a whisper, I plopped my butt heavily onto the concrete.

TWELVE

The square-jawed police officer turned out to be a decent fellow. Officer Brad Beck could've given us a ticket for any one of a number of things, like speeding, reckless driving or even littering, but he didn't. Instead, after we spent the next hour cleaning up the debris that used to be Crazy Climber, he invited us to have a cup of coffee and some breakfast at a small all-night diner owned by him and his wife Julie. Sitting on uncomfortable barstools at the Cop Shop Diner, we told the Becks all about our travels. "Oh my," Julie said, her eyes clearly tearing up, "you came all this way, spent all that money to buy the game, only to have it end like this. That's horrible."

"You're telling us," Austin replied.

Officer Beck sat on an adjacent barstool, sipping a still-steaming cup of black coffee. "Are you sure you don't want to press charges on those men? They are directly responsible for destruction of your property and they could've seriously injured you two. You have every right."

I sat with my hands on my cheeks, elbows on either side of my coffee cup. The steam heat wafting over my chin gave me a small amount of comfort, for some reason. "No. I know I should, but I'm exhausted and utterly crushed. And we don't ever wanna have to come back here. No offense." After pausing to take a sip of coffee, I continued, "I was so proud of us on this journey. We made it nearly three thousand miles with no money, using only our wits and the kindness of strangers, only to have it end like this. It's so disheartening."

"We just wanna go home." Austin tipped his glass up in the air, the ice cubes from his Coke clinking against his teeth. The man never got into coffee.

"I can understand that, boys. I'm still going to have a nice, long chat with Frank Wanker. Oh and no matter what, I am gonna need your contact information."

After giving the officer our info, I turned to my comrade. "Well Austin, we should get home. Do we have any money left?"

He shook his head, then opened his mouth to speak when Julie shouted, "Oh no! This is on the house. And not only that, but here." With that, she handed us a twenty-dollar bill. "Use this for gas."

Though I had every intention of turning down her generous offer, I simply didn't have it in me. Instead, an errant tear rolled down my cheek. Going from the worst of humanity in the Wanker clan to the best with these wonderful, generous people, I think my last shred of stability gave way. Through my abject despair, I forced a smile and pocketed the cash, thanking them wholeheartedly. It took all of my willpower not to turn into a blubbering mess right there on the spot.

With the Crazy pieces dumped in the back of the truck, we hit a gas station, filled the tank and drove straight home. The conversation was minimal in those final hours of travel. Not having much to say, we just stared straight ahead and watched the miles tick down to zero.

Once we reached Austin's house, I pulled in his driveway and idled. He turned and patted my shoulder, the closest I believe we've ever come to an embrace. "Well my friend, it sure ended suckily, but despite what I said earlier, I kinda enjoyed this adventure."

A smile squeaked out from the edges of my mouth. "It did have its moments, didn't it?"

"It's something I'll never forget. I'm glad you invited me along."

"Me too, pal. Me too."

He pushed Ol' Red's door open and stepped out. Turning back to look me in the eye, he added, "If you ever wanna do something like this again someday, let me know."

After nodding my agreement, I rolled on home, emptied the Crazy debris into the garage and wandered inside.

Upon entering, I let out a gasp. My place looked quite disheveled, with my wastebasket and end tables knocked over, and all my plants torn up. There was plant dirt and trash everywhere. Moments later, my cat came bounding up to me, mewing like a spurned girlfriend. Scooping her in my arms, I scratched her head while I wandered around the place. "Geez Heidi, I see you missed me."

With my foot, I flipped one of my end tables over and saw my answering machine blinking away. Setting her down, I bent over and pushed the play button. Instantly, I heard Phil's anxious voice. "Jay, where are you? You were supposed to be back yesterday. I trust you had no problem with Ol' Red. Call me, man!"

When the second message started playing more of Phil's voice, I quickly turned the machine off. Oh, I had no interest in dealing with that situation right now.

Heidi wouldn't stop assaulting me with her caterwauling, so I looked down and waggled my finger at her. "We'll have a chat in the morning about the damage you caused, young lady. But for now, I need to sleep." I left the bedroom door open, and she curled up next to me. The little hellion didn't stop purring before I fell asleep.

After a much-deserved night's rest in my own bed, I woke up feeling a little bit better. Rolling over, I saw Heidi next to me, curled up in a tight ball. I doubt she left my side all night.

I put it off for most of the day, but eventually, I worked up the nerve to wander into the garage to start playing around with the pieces of my arcade machine.

The case and monitor were totaled, of course. No amount of duct tape and super glue would do any good there. Also, I couldn't even find the power cord. In my mind's eye, I could see it still attached to the extension cord plugged in to Wanker's socket. But, as it turned out, I would be able to replace it easily. It simply snapped off from the power supply. Once I located a generic cord and spliced it in, the power supply powered right up. Even the speaker still worked. I had certainly lucked out there.

Also, amazingly, the circuitry was in a lot better shape than I thought possible. The case apparently took the brunt of the shock, and once it shattered, all the pieces took flight like iron butterflies in the steel breeze. Contact with the pavement loosened some chips and unseated others, but other than a few soldering tasks, everything tested okay, to my amazement. So, from what I could tell, that meant I simply needed to purchase a monitor and a cabinet. "I wonder where to look," I said to no one as I dashed inside to my computer.

A quick online search revealed someone selling a Crazy Climber cabinet in Florida. After contacting the guy, I also found out he had a spare monitor, so I ordered that as well. Unfortunately, I'd have to do some more traveling. Sheesh.

"Uhhh. Hullo," Austin replied after around twenty-five rings.

"Hey Austy, it's Jay. What're ya doing for the next week?"

"Huh?"

Randy D Pearson

THIRTEEN

Austin exhaled a large, exaggerated sigh. "Florida, now? Really? Ya couldn't find one in Michigan? Ya know, I'll bet someone in Lansing has a cabinet collecting dust in their basement."

I had to smile at that. "Oh sure, you're probably right. Even though it's an obsolete, outdated game that very few people even remember, I'm sure there's a spare cabinet right around the corner. Heck, the neighbor's probably got one right now. Let me go check." Pausing momentarily for comedic effect, I continued, "Dang it, he just sold it to a guy in Florida. What're the odds?"

"Funny, dude."

"I know. I'm a laugh riot. Besides, I already bought and paid for it with PayPal."

Austin's silence worried me a bit, but I knew he had to think it through. "I dunno, man. Frankly, I don't think I'm up for another road trip so soon. I'm surprised you are, to be honest."

"Yeah, I hear ya. But the way I look at it, we did have fun. And I need this to end differently. If we give up now, the Wankers of the world win. It just doesn't sit right, y'know."

"The Wankers of the world, Jay? How long's that line been floating around in your noggin?"

I thought about lying, but why bother? "Oh, for hours, of course. Besides, this time will be different. I'll hit the bank and pull lots of cash from my savings, I'll have my credit card, and..." A firecracker went off in my head. "Dang it!"

"What?"

"Geez, I completely forgot about my stolen credit card, again. I never did cancel that thing. Crap!"

"Oh man! I'll bet she maxed ya out. Just imagine all the stuff she now owns on your dime. She probably bought a car, a house, and a yacht. Oh, the possibilities!" Friends can be so cruel.

"Ya can't buy a house with a credit card. At least not my card. Fortunately, the bank didn't trust me with a very high limit. Good call on their part, in retrospect. But I'll call Visa after I hang up with you." After a quick pause, I added, "So anyway, the thing's already paid for, and I'm going in the morning. Ya wanna come along? Please say yes, please say yes."

Austin breathed out another overly-dramatic sigh. "Well, hell, I guess. I don't have anything better to do. I don't have a job anymore. But you do. How're ya gonna get off work this time?"

Man, I hadn't thought of that, either. Our last trip, somehow, managed to take exactly two weeks. They were expecting me back bright and early Monday morning ... tomorrow. Well, actually, I should've been back last Monday, so now I gotta finagle an extra week plus smooth over the AWOL week. "I don't know. I'll think of something. All right, I'll call ya back."

At least I had the rest of the day to come up with some foolproof plan to get out of another week of work. But while I milled that around in my mind, I figured the Visa people would have reps available on a Sunday afternoon. So, I rummaged around in my Important Document Pile and managed to locate an old bill.

"Please hold, your call is very important to us." After several minutes of that typical drivel on a loop, a man with a thick Middle Eastern accent came on the line. He started by identifying himself as Sam. "How can I be helping you today, Jaymond Naylor?"

Though horribly stereotypical of me, I didn't expect his name to be Sam. Sanjay or Mohinder I would've bought. I almost said something about it, but fortunately, I thought better of it. "Yes, uh, Sam. I had my credit card stolen last week, while on vacation. Can you tell me what's been charged to it since Wednesday, June third?"

Holding my breath while I heard him typing, my mind flashed back to that pretty, drunk girl in that seedy Nashville bar. Again, I know stereotypes rarely fit, especially as we near the turn of the century, but she didn't look like a thief to me. Of course, as I thought it, I realized how dumb I sounded. What, did I expect her to don a Lone Ranger-style mask or a black-and-white striped shirt? I can be so naïve sometimes.

"Okay Mr. Naylor," Sam said matter-of-factly, "fortunately, there aren't many charges. There's only

$218.12 in purchases since the third. It appears to be primarily grocery stores and restaurants. Just food and clothing. In fact," he said with a noticeable pause, "your card was used each of the last two Wednesdays and Saturdays at a store called MegaShop in Nashville. I'll go ahead and cancel your card as of today and credit those charges back to you. We'll be mailing you a police report in the coming days. Just fill it out and we'll take care of the rest."

Well, that was easier than I anticipated. "Thank you, Sam. You're all right." Then, a thought struck me. "One more thing. Can you give me the address of that MegaShop in Nashville?"

## FOURTEEN

Early Monday morning, I felt my heart beating in my chest as I made the phone call.

"Millen and Billman. How may I direct your call?"

"Bertha in HR, please."

When the manly-voiced Bertha answered, I completely lost my game plan. Crap, my mind went blank! "Oh, uh, hi Bertha. It's Jay Naylor. Say, uh, I won't be able to make it in this week, either."

"Hmph. And why is that, Jay?" After a few audible key clicks, she continued. "It says here you were at your grandmother's funeral for...the last two weeks. You only requested one week off of work."

"Uh, yeah, about that. Turned out she didn't actually die of...the pork gout. It was just a, uh, gout

131

coma. She came out of it late last week. So y'know, we were all mighty relieved. But then, uh, Grandpapa, we call him that, y'know, Grandpapa caught it and now he's in the coma."

"Excuse me? A gout coma? You can't even catch gout."

"Yeah, uh, I don't know what to tell ya, but I guess pork gout is contagious. Who knew? I'm not a doctor, after all. All I know is, the family really needs me. So, one more week, in our time of need. I'll be back next Monday for sure. I promise."

Her prolonged pause really caused the sweat to ooze down my forehead. "Okay Jay, I'll put you down for one more week off. But understand, you only asked for one week of vacation in the first place, so you have five days of 'no-call/no-shows' on your record. You might not have a job when you come back."

"I understand. There are no guarantees in this world. Heck, I might end up infected myself. If it happens, Bertha, if I catch the gout, remember me fondly." I hung up before she could respond. Breathing a sigh of relief, I whispered, "Gout coma, Jay? Geez, I'm a nitwit."

Certainly not the smartest thing I'd ever done, jeopardizing a job of several years for a bloody video game cabinet. But heck, they loved me there. I'd still have a job when I return. Probably.

In the late morning, after a quick load of laundry, I walked out to Ol' Red with my duffel bag in hand. When I approached the Chevy S-10, I had a massive panic attack. In all my haste to get inside, collapse into a deep sleep and then deal with Crazy in my closed garage, I had neglected to even take a good look at Phil's pickup truck.

Good Lord, did those bikers do a number on it! Both sides had massive scrapes and dents from the Wanker clan's vicious attack. Several nasty indentations littered the bed wall, and black paint streaks lined both sides from the door to the tailgate. They even managed to pockmark the top of the cab and the hood. Walking the length of Ol' Red, I dragged my hand along the surface, up and down the craters. "Wow, you poor thing."

At least I could feel a small amount of pride in having added some fresh war wounds to the Wankermobile. In reality, it probably didn't matter one way or the other, but the thought made me feel a tiny bit better.

Then, my thoughts fell to the owner of Ol' Red. Phil might not kill me, but he certainly wouldn't be pleased over this turn of events. I knew I had to tell him, and quite honestly, I really needed to ask for permission to borrow it for another week. But the old saying, 'It's better to ask for forgiveness than permission' came sharply to mind, and I reluctantly chose not to call. Besides, I reasoned, I certainly didn't want to bother him at work. It would annoy him. Using that twisted logic as my touchstone, I packed up the pickup and headed over to snag Austin.

I knew better than to assume Austin would be ready to leave when I arrived. Heck, the chances of his being awake had to be minimal. After pounding on his door for a couple of minutes, I reached in my pocket for the key he gave me a couple weeks ago. Cursing under my breath, I realized I probably left it in the pocket of one of my other pairs of jeans, stuffed in my duffel bag. Or heck, it could be lying in the bottom of the washer, for all I knew.

Luckily for me, I remembered his hidden spare key. With my dear friend, I knew I merely had to look for the fake rock in a well-trampled area. When we lived together, Austin locked his keys in the house at least once a month on average. Sure enough, the tall, flattened weeds practically pointed to his key's hiding spot like a searchlight.

Upon entering his house, I listened for the snoring. "Ah yes, thar she blows!" I trampled up the stairs and rousted the sleeping troll.

While waiting for him to get ready, I went out and got us breakfast. "Mickey D's, the breakfast of champions," I announced while holding the bag in the air, "and I got you a Coke."

This time, I let Austin sleep as we made our way down the highway, allowing myself time to think. For the last couple of weeks, I had been running pretty much on instinct and adrenaline, reacting to situations as they arose. In contrast, my life before this adventure had been much more structured, with a lot less risk-taking. Moderation and planning were my non-verbalized mantras.

Heck, I might not even have a job when I returned home. This realization should've filled me to the brim with panic and trepidation. But instead, it felt oddly liberating. Okay, fine, but why wasn't I concerned? Did this trip somehow change me? Sure, I got in a bar fight, drank with teenagers around a campfire and even got lucky on a pool table, but did that somehow alter my viewpoint?

Well, before this, I guess I was content to stay in my sheltered little world, only interacting with my tiny core of friends. I had my restaurant, my bar and my coffee shop. Altering my daily activities made me uneasy. These last two weeks opened my eyes to other possibilities, I suppose.

But what if we run into more bad guys? That whole Wanker thing definitely scared me to my core. But on the other hand, I got chased by a bloodthirsty mob and lived to tell the tale.

Not only that, but regardless of the consequences, I found myself back on the road again, blasting into the unknown. Oddly enough, I realized I had no trepidation about how this leg of our journey would unfold. Yes, we might run into more Wankers, but at least this time, I felt better prepared. Reaching into my duffel bag, I felt around until my fingers caressed the smooth aluminum of my little league baseball bat. I removed the bat and slid it under Ol' Red's bench seat. Whether or not I'd have the guts to use it, only time would tell. With any luck, I wouldn't have to find out.

After several hours, Austin slowly stirred and finally awoke. Stretching, he uttered, "Man, I can't believe I let you talk me into this again."

"Road trip!" I yelled with a grin. "I know, but this time, it'll be more of a vacation. I have several hundred dollars, and in several different locations on my person and in my belongings. So, no one's gonna pilfer all my cash this time. We can stay in Florida for a couple of days, see the sights, check out the beach babes!" I added a wink to that last statement. "And here's a fun idea. We're going to stop off in Nashville on the way down."

Austin turned sharply to gape at me. "Uh, and why would that be fun?"

"This time, we can be tourists. It's the home of country music, after all. We can stop at the Grand Olde Opry, maybe visit Graceland."

Gazing at the side of my head with a dumfounded look, he said, "Dude, we both hate country music and Elvis."

Though I tried to suppress it, that comment made me snicker. "Okay, ya got me. I managed to get some interesting news about the chick that stole my credit card. She's been shopping at the same store on the same days. We're gonna go to that store and track her down. Fun, right?"

"Good Lord, dude, have you gone mental? The chances of us being there at the exact time as her have got to be astronomical. What if she has a gang or something?"

"A gang? Come on!"

"We don't know. She could be part of a giant group of thieves. A biker gang, the mob, it could be anything."

A boisterous laugh escaped from deep inside of me. "Do you hear yourself? The mob? Really? You know how ridiculous you sound?"

"Me, ridiculous? I mean really Jay, what good can possibly come from this plan? What do you hope to accomplish?"

He had me on that one. "I dunno. I guess I just want to approach her and make her feel guilty. Maybe I can get my money back, but if nothing else, I want her to face me. Besides," I added with a smile, "we're already en route." Without his knowledge, I switched expressways.

"Freakin' lovely," he replied. "Then yes, we are definitely going to Graceland. I, er, kinda like Elvis." He gave me a sheepish grin.

"So what, are ya all shook up?"

"Well, you're nothing but a hound dog."

"Well you're... uh, wearing blue suede shoes."

"Weak, dude. Totally weak."

"I know. But in my defense, I only make jokes like that once in a blue moon."

"Stop it. Just stop it."

Since we weren't in any sort of a hurry, we decided to cease our travels early for the first day in southern Indiana. The green road signs had three choices, but one in particular caught my attention. "Oh, how cool! Let's stop at Shelbyville."

"Why? What's so cool about Shelbyville?"

I flashed Austin a toothy grin. "It's the name of Springfield's arch nemesis town."

"What?"

"From the Simpsons."

My friend shook his head slowly. "Dude, you're such a dork."

"And proud of it," I replied gleefully.

This time, having the resources, we chose to stay someplace a bit more respectable. We found ourselves a sanitary-looking Vacation Inn and booked us a room.

Once we dumped our luggage in our roach-free room, we headed straight to the attached bar. "This," I told Austin as we clinked our rum and Coke glasses together, "is what we missed the first time. Look at this place, will ya?"

"Sure is clean." He clearly wasn't on board yet, and he probably still had reservations about my plan to confront the pickpocket. But that wouldn't happen for another couple of days, so for now, I wanted to live it up a little.

"Well, there's a shocker," I said with a chuckle, "lookee over there." Pointing at the far wall until Austin paid attention to me, he saw the Galaga machine and cracked a smile. "Ya had to know I wouldn't book a room unless it had a Galaga machine nearby." Of course, I had no clue about the proximity of any arcade games. But heck, why shouldn't I take the credit? "C'mon, I'll challenge you to a game. Winner buys the next round."

That made him laugh boisterously. "Nice try there, dude. Loser, that'll be you, will buy me my next rum and Coke."

We played a couple games of Galaga, with Austin winning both times, naturally. Then, we moved on to the pool table. Even though we both pretty much sucked at it, I had the upper hand early on. I've always had what I call beginner's luck. With most games I haven't played in a while, I can do well initially, until my innate loserness kicks in and I falter.

While waiting on Austin to attempt a bank shot, I scanned the bar. It being a Monday, the place had only a few patrons. The couple in the far booth, sitting extremely close to one another, probably had an interesting story. The man looked to be in his fifties or even older, with completely gray hair, practically white in the ambient lighting. His wrinkles had been gouged deeply into his cheeks and forehead, like glaciers cutting a swath across the land back in the ice age. The woman, by contrast, had to be barely legal, with smooth, chocolate skin and a short skirt showing off beautiful, curvy legs. Was he cheating on his wife, I wondered? Could that be his secretary? I know it sounded cliché, but my mind went there first.

Being so enthralled with those two, I didn't notice the woman approaching us. When she rested her hands directly between us on the pool table, she startled me. Her long, platinum blonde hair cascaded past her shoulders, dangling just above the table as she leaned slightly forward. "Hello fellas," she said with a soft, breezy voice, "can I play the winner?" Standing a couple inches shorter than either of us, she wore a white, button-down shirt with the top two buttons undone, and a denim jean skirt, showing off a pair of legs she had undoubtedly worked hard to sculpt.

Before I could answer, Austin loudly smacked the cue ball into the eight, sinking it in the right corner pocket. He shot her a slick smile. "That would be me, and yes, yes you can, darlin'."

I gave him a long, deep bow before taking a couple steps back. Plopping down on a barstool at the closest table, I said, "I'm Jay, and the winner over there is Austin."

"But you can call me Flash." Austin's smile grew imperceptibly.

"I don't know why you'd want to," I muttered under my breath.

"That's funny, Austin. I'll withhold judgment on Flash for the moment. My name's Maggy."

She held out her right hand, and my suave friend took it gently, cupping it with both of his own. "Is it short for Magnolia? Because if it's not, it should be."

"Pretty as a flower," I added, but she didn't take her eyes off him.

Austin started the game out with a clean break, sinking the red three. From there, they traded shots and the conversation flowed. I tried to interject once or twice, but for whatever reason, she barely noticed me. So, I decided to concede. Neither of us generally had much luck in situations like these, so kudos to him. Besides, I guess it was his turn. The memory of another pool table still held fresh in my mind. Still, I couldn't help but feel more than a little slighted.

I finished my drink and moseyed up to the bar, plopping down next to a man who appeared to be a career alcoholic. He had some of the telltale signs, like the gin blossoms sprouting across his nose, the dull sheen in his eyes, and the thick bags under those lifeless orbs. Oh, and the nine empty shot glasses, aligned upside-down in a nearly completed pyramid, gave me a subtle clue. I whistled as I sat next to him on a wobbly bar stool. "Nice stacking job."

"Takes a steady hand," he replied, "and years of practice."

"I know I don't have the skill set. Hell, I couldn't drink that many shots of anything."

"That also takes practice." He looked me up and down before continuing. "Where ya from, bub?"

"Is it that obvious I'm not local?"

"Well, you're at a hotel bar, and I'm about the only regular that comes in here, so yeah."

"Okay, sure. Keen insight. I'm from Lansing, Michigan. My buddy and I are headed to Florida to pick up a video game cabinet."

"Bah," he said after tipping back his tenth shot of Jack Daniels, "video games are for children. Ya want a real game, try Mumblety-Peg."

I shot him a queer glance. "Uh, you mean that knife game where ya put your hand flat on the table and you stab between the fingers?"

"No, ya mook, that's Five Finger Fillet. Here," he continued as he slid off his barstool. He put both feet on the ground and once he steadied himself, he pulled out a formidable pocketknife. In one shockingly quick motion, he snapped open the four-inch blade and tossed it abruptly, sinking it in the wood floor about two inches from his right foot. "Eh, not bad. Now, it's your turn."

As he closed his blade and handed it to me, I could feel my anxiety welling up. "Uh, you want me to toss this knife at your foot?"

He shook his head slowly. "Not my foot, bub. Your foot." He stared at me in anticipation, a small smile curling his lips upward.

Surely, my face grew flush as I thought about this insane activity. Oh sure, let me toss a knife at my foot. I'll get right on that.

Fortunately for me, the bartender saw the events unfolding and snatched the closed knife from my grasp. "Mel, I'm not gonna tell you again. Keep your damn blade in your pocket or I'm cutting you off. Got it?"

"Bah. Fine, ya mook. Besides, this wuss wouldn't have had the stones to do it, anyway."

After flashing the bartender a quick, relieved smile, I turned back to Mel. "I guess we'll never know."

"We could always take it to the parking lot," he said with an evil grin.

I shook my head rapidly and held up both hands, showing Mel the palms of my hands in the universal sign for surrender. "Okay fine, I guess we do know. You win."

Once we got our knife fight out of the way, and I'd put a couple more rum and Cokes in me, Mel and I got to talking about Y2K. "Frankly," he said as he started adding a fifth row on his pyramid, "I could give a rat's ass about what'll happen after 2000. As long as I can get a case of Jack and a few tins of chew, I'll do just fine. Besides, I got my knife, my guns and plenty of ammo. I'll live off the land. The deer won't stop working, and neither will I."

After a while, I felt a slap on my back. I turned to find Austin and Maggy standing behind me, arm in arm. "Jay, we're gettin' outta here. I'll be back in the morning. Don't leave without me." Part of me screamed with raging jealously. I mean, why him? Why not me? But no, he needed this more than I did. I couldn't remember him ever getting lucky in a bar.

Faking my best genuine-looking smile, I said, "All right, man, have fun. I'd like to get rollin' by noon."

"Yeah, shouldn't be a problem. Oh hey," he added as he tossed a thumb at the bathroom. "I gotta hit the head. Keep her company for a minute, would ya?" I shrugged as he turned and bolted away.

Maggy stared at me for a moment. "You don't hide your jealousy well, y'know."

This floored me. Talk about being direct! "What are you talking about?"

She leaned closer to me and spoke clearly. "In twenty minutes of conversation, I learned a lot about Austin. We spent some time talking about his divorce. Which, when you think about it, is probably the worst way to try to pick up a girl in a bar. I'm just a sucker for a sob story, I guess. But you know how he's been feeling...betrayed, lost, lonely. He loved her more than he thought possible, and she completely blindsided him. It devastated the poor guy. He puts on a brave face, but he's a mess inside. I reckon that's why I'm taking him home. This is something Austin has clearly needed for a long time. So be happy for your friend."

Wow, she learned all that in twenty minutes? Fortunately, Austin returned from the bathroom at that moment, since I had no idea what to say to her after that. So, when Austin threw his arm around her shoulder, I nodded to him then turned to her. "Pleasure meeting you, Maggy."

"You too, Jeff." I bristled at that, and thought about correcting her, but I kept it internal. She turned to my friend and whispered, "Let's go, Flash." As they left the bar, she turned her head and winked at me.

Wow, that Austin, what a lucky bastard. Apparently, he did everything wrong and still got the girl. I guess that old saying had some merit, the one about nuts and blind squirrels.

Though I knew he wouldn't be back by noon, I still had a bit of annoyance creep into me as time ticked by. I kept reminding myself we didn't need to rush. Actually, this worked out better. It would only take a few hours to get to Nashville from here. Arriving at a decent time Tuesday night, we would be able to get a good night's sleep, allowing us all day for my MegaShop stakeout on Wednesday.

Finally, at a bit after three o'clock, Austin came sauntering in. "S'up."

"S'up yourself, Flash. So, was it everything you'd hoped for?"

Grinning like a complete idiot, he breathed, "Ohhhh, yeah. I needed that."

"Good, good. So, ya wanna hit the road now, or do you need to, y'know, freshen up, delouse, something?"

Laughing, he said, "You're a riot when you're jealous."

Though on the money, I still felt it best to deny everything. "Ah, I have no need to be jealous. I already had my fun last week. I never did tell ya about me and Mistress Jackie making it on her pool table. Unlike you, I didn't want to brag."

My friend continued to laugh, and actually chuckled a bit louder as he pulled a clean shirt from his suitcase. "Okay Jay, believe whatever fantasy you need, to make you feel like a man."

"Oh, but it's not a fanta…" As he wandered into the bathroom and closed the door, I decided to drop it. It didn't matter if he believed or not. To end this conversation, I yelled, "Whatever. Just remember, next time it'll be my turn!"

He popped the door open and leaned around the frame. "Hey man, I can't help it if the ladies dig the Flashdrive."

That caused a loud groan to slip out of me. "Flashdrive. Great."

Once Flash made himself presentable, we hit a small diner to get our feed on. After my lunch and his breakfast, we were back on the road, to Nashville.

Several uneventful hours later, we arrived in the place they called Music City. After being spoiled at the last Vacation Inn, we treated ourselves to a suite at another one. Austin whistled as he looked around the nice, clean room. "Hey," he said with a grin, "check this out!" In one swift motion, he tossed his suitcase onto the closest bed. "Nothing scampered off. No bugs!"

Walking over to the other bed, I kneeled while slowly lifting up the bedspread, to glance under the bed. "And there's only one dead hooker under here. This must be what heaven's like."

"Oh, c'mon dude, there's no dead hookers in heaven."

"What about the hooker with a heart of gold?"

"Purgatory at best."

"Oh ye of little faith."

Feeling like I had karma on my side, we pulled into the parking lot of the MegaShop supermarket. Then, I saw the size of the building. As we stood at one of the many entrances, looking up at the massive structure, Austin said casually, "Kinda reminds me of Meijer."

"No, it's not that big. More like a Kroger. Or maybe that L & L on Logan Street."

"Still, it's big."

"Uh-huh. Bigger than I had hoped."

We entered the establishment, automatic doors welcoming us inside. "So Jay, what's the plan here?"

"Plan?" Well, I suppose a plan would've been a good idea. "I guess we shop for a while." I gestured to my right. "You go down that aisle, and I'll head to the other end of the store. We'll meet in the middle."

"Uh, yeah. Great plan, genius, except for one small flaw."

"What's that?"

"I never saw her. She vamoosed before I ever laid eyes on her, remember?"

Crap! "Oh yeah. Well, if you see a cute young chick, this tall," I rested my hand just under my nose, "with long, auburn hair, come get me."

Austin furrowed his brow. "Auburn?"

Oh, right. Like most men, he could only see in primary colors. "Just look for brown hair."

Shaking his head slowly, Austin replied, "Oh sure, this'll go well."

"Oh ye of little faith. Ooo, déjà vu!"

Pacing up one aisle and down the next, I scanned the crowd laboriously for quite some time. Once I'd wandered through my whole section with no results, I opted instead to pick a location and hover. Perusing the fresh fruits and vegetables section, I feigned fascination in their selection of cucumbers, strawberries and broccoli. I'd pick up an item and do all sorts of freshness quality testing, or at least what I'd hoped would be construed as such. For any given item, I'd smell, thump or shake it, only to return it to, or in the general vicinity of, its original location. Though I did garner some peculiar glances while shaking broccoli near my ear and smelling sealed bags of salad, I think I managed to fool the majority of the shoppers.

I repeated these tasks for about an hour before attracting the attention of the produce manager, an overweight man with an enormous nose and puffy pink cheeks. Though I knew someone was hovering near me, I didn't actually take notice until his nose's elongated shadow fell over the oranges I simulated interest in. I spun around, orange in hand, as he said, "Can I help you with anything, sir?"

I looked the man up and down before responding. "No thanks. Just checking the freshness of these oranges. I've got it covered. Thanks, though." I dismissed him with a backhanded wave, then tapped the orange with my knuckle and held it to my ear like a seashell.

My quality testing caused his brow to furrow. "You don't thump oranges, sir. That's for melons."

"Yeah, well, this is how they do it in Australia. You telling me the Aussies are wrong here?"

"If what you say is true, then yes. Thumping an orange won't tell you if it's fresh."

Though this amused me, I made a point of displaying a curmudgeonly countenance. "Okay then, why don't you inform me, oh guru of groceries, how I'm supposed to tell if this orange is any good."

Snatching it from my grasp, he held it equidistant between us. "You look at it, for one. There's no bruising, except where you've been hitting it. Otherwise, it's uniform in color. Also," he added while holding it under his nose, "if it smells nice and juicy, it is a good orange."

I seized it back from him, resting it under my own nose. "Well, I clearly don't have your formidable tools, but I'll give it a go." The man's eyes narrowed enough to confirm he got my huge honker joke. "I dunno, man. It smells bruised to me."

"It doesn't smell bruised! What does that even mean?"

"It means I'm not buying it." Putting it back on the pile, I picked up another one, put it next to my ear and began shaking it. "Now this one, yes. This one sounds ripe."

Clearly becoming agitated, the manager spouted, "Sounds ripe?! What are you talking about? You don't shake oranges, either."

I shook my head in mock disgust. "Oh, you poor, uneducated man. How ever did you get this job?"

Just as his face flushed an unhealthy shade of crimson, a loud crash emanated from a few aisles away. Off in the distance, I could clearly detect Austin's voice, then a woman shouting an obscenity-laced tirade in a shrill, piercing tone. I flipped the orange in the air, causing ol' big nose to lunge at it in a panic. "Well, this has been enlightening, for you, but I've gotta go." Without awaiting a response, I dashed away from the agitated produce manager.

When I arrived at the commotion, I found Austin sprawled on the tiled floor, yelling up at a short, obese ogre of a woman. I quickly yanked him to his feet. "What's going on here, buddy? This isn't the woman, y'know."

Oh, the glare he gave me could've melted ice... or steel, for that matter. "Good Lord, I hope not! I'd have to stop being your friend. No, this troll slammed into me, and now she's screaming at me as if it's my fault."

She jabbed her meaty index finger at him. "You ran into me, you idiot! You came sprinting around the corner and plowed right into me. Good thing I'm sturdy, otherwise you would've knocked me over."

"Oh, sturdy is not the word I'd use. I'd say you're more..."

Raising my hand and putting it directly in front of my friend's face, I quickly cut him off. No good could possibly come from the end of that sentence. "Dude, shush. Ma'am, sorry for the trouble. Are you okay?" Looking into her cart, I couldn't help but add, "Did he damage your lifetime supply of Ding-Dongs?"

Her eyes threw daggers at me for a moment, but instead of replying, she pulled her cart away and began pushing it in the opposite direction. "You're just lucky I'm a lady."

"I'd say the lady you devoured wasn't so lucky," Austin retorted, "ya fat old..."

In a surprisingly quick motion, the woman spun around and hit Austin in the head with her massive purse. The blow propelled him into me, clunking our heads together in a Three Stooges kind of maneuver. While we bounced off the shelf and tumbled to the ground, she snorted and resumed shoving her cart away. A sizeable crowd had formed and several of them chuckled at our embarrassing scene. Austin touched the side of his head, and once he was convinced he hadn't sustained any external injury, said loudly, "Okay folks, nothing to see here. Move along."

I added, "The next show's at three. Tip your waitress." Then, I rubbed the side of my head. "Ow. Man, what was that all about?"

"Dude, I think I found your little thief when I plowed into that heifer. She might still be here, if we hurry. C'mon!" He pulled himself to his feet, helped me up, and we both dashed down the bread aisle. "Okay, I saw her here, with a cart. I think she was headed that way." He pointed in the opposite direction.

We sprinted through several aisles until we came upon a short, auburn haired woman with her back to us, checking out a can of Campbell's Chunky Chicken Corn Chowder soup. Dashing up to her, I dropped my hand heavily on her shoulder. "Aha! I caught you!"

Some woman I had never seen before turned around and whacked me in the shoulder with the can of soup. After dropping the now-dented can, she released a blood-curdling scream. My buddy and I bolted away from her at lightning speed.

It didn't take long after that incident before the management caught up to us and politely informed us that we were hereby banned from all MegaShop grocery stores in the future. While they escorted us from the premises, I felt the need to have the last word. "Yeah, well, I'd never shop here again anyway. Your oranges are too bruisey! And don't get me started on the state of your broccoli!"

Not in my wildest dreams would I have imagined I'd ever be back here again, at Bob's Country Palace, my shoes still sticking to the floor. But after we spent the past several hours walking, running and falling around MegaShop, I needed to sit and have some food. Even though across the street there loomed a nice looking family-type restaurant called Lenny's Diner, I really needed a stiff drink as well. And, of course, I had ulterior motives for wanting to be here. "Well," Austin said as we sat down at the same table we did two weeks ago, "there's three hours we'll never get back. But at least my head's stopped aching. How are your abrasions?"

A sigh escaped my pursed lips. "Well, your head somewhat softened the big woman's blow, but the soup punch will definitely leave a bruise. But yeah, I'll be okay." I paused to rub my shoulder for a moment. "Man, I felt so sure that thieving wench would show up there, with my credit card in hand. I was certain karma would be on my side for this one."

"Karma's a fickle mistress, Dude. Besides, the place was gigantic. She could've easily been there, in and out, and we might've never even seen her. It was a losing proposition. I tried to tell ya, but would you listen? No."

"I know. Crap."

Looking around at our surroundings, Austin said with a laughing snort, "Oh, and I suppose we're in this fine establishment only because the food's so darn scrumptious?"

We even got the same surly waitress from last time, and she stomped toward us as I quietly replied, "That and the top-notch service-with-a-snarl."

I half-expected her to say something like, "Oh, it's you two again," but that would've meant she paid attention to her customers. No, I rather doubted that.

Even before she opened her mouth, I spouted, "Two beers, two burgers." She nearly cracked a grin at that, but said nothing as she nodded her comprehension of our order. It kinda felt like a *Groundhog Day* moment, that Bill Murray movie from a few years back.

Austin half-heartedly scanned the bar. "Okay, fine. So we're here, two weeks after your card was stolen. Do you see her around anywhere?"

I put my head on a swivel, checking every table, chair and barstool. "Nah. I guess that would've been too easy."

We sat in that crap hole for numerous hours, drinking beer and playing video games. I managed to beat Austin in a game of Tempest, which gave me a momentary hurrah. Also, I did have a woman hit on me, but she had to be in her 60s and smelled like whiskey, talcum powder and denture adhesive. For some reason, this wrinkled old prune thought her removable teeth would be a selling point. When she dislodged them from her mouth, placing them in her open palm, I nearly spewed my beer. "Oh, I'm sorry," I told her, "but I'm a lesbian. Can't help it. It's how I'm wired."

She gave me a puzzled look, but it got her to mosey away, so victory for me.

After several more hours, we had had enough. Of course, Austin wanted to give up even before we arrived, but I had also finally reached my wit's end. I had to face the facts and realize I would not be getting my revenge.

Funny, when the word *revenge* hit my mind, I realized I truly had no idea what it meant to me. What point *did* I have in wanting to confront her? Would I have attacked her and taken my money back, hauled her off to the police station or bought her a drink and listened to her story? Since I clearly had no strategy, not finding her was probably for the best, anyway.

As Austin wandered off to the bathroom, I paid our tab. At that moment, out of the corner of my eye, I spotted a small, longhaired woman walk in from the street. I did a quick double take. She looked exactly the same as she did two weeks ago, the tiny lady with those high cheekbones, auburn hair and that seductively sly smile.

Even though I had been waiting in anticipation of this moment, I still had no idea what to say or do. I felt my heart thumping wildly in my chest and I started involuntarily blushing, for some reason. As she wandered up to the counter and sat on a barstool, I glanced back at the bathroom. Austin hadn't emerged yet. Being fairly toasted after all the beers of the evening, I decided to wing it. Plan, who needs a plan? I mean, why change now, right?

Sauntering up behind her, I exhaled heavily before speaking to the back of her head. "Hey baby, remember me?"

She turned, and her coy smile instantly evaporated. Oh, she remembered me, all right. She spun quickly and gave me a shove as she launched herself off the stool and sprinted toward the door.

Quickly giving pursuit, I followed her out the door. I found it a bit odd, amusing even, that no one in the bar seemed to care. At the very least, I'd have thought someone would've been chivalrous enough to try to help, but maybe she'd scammed enough of the locals here that she'd lost all favor. Or perhaps Nashville was the *Mind Your Own Business* City? I made a mental note to check the city limits sign on the way out of town.

The pretty brunette dashed a few steps away from the bar before running headlong into another patron. The impact knocked her to the ground, landing her on her derriere with a dusty thud. When I realized Austin had bolted out the back door and come around front to meet us, I shot him a quick nod and a grin.

As she jumped back to her feet, her eyes rapidly darting between Austin and me, I quickly yelled, "Stop! Now look, we are going to have a conversation, just the three of us. You owe me that much, and you know it."

Slowly backing away from me, she tried her best to produce a puzzled facade. "What? Do I know you?"

Instinctively, Austin stopped her from inching off by resting his hands on her shoulder. Normally, neither of us could even begin to overpower anyone, but we had the advantage due to her diminutive stature. We both probably towered a good six inches over her.

"Stop playing games with me, woman. You know damn well who I am, or you wouldn't have run away like that."

She rolled her eyes at me and sighed. "Fine, whatever. So what do you want? I don't have your money anymore. I spent it all. It wasn't much. And the card stopped working, so I tossed it."

"Yeah, that's fine. I figured that. Actually, I'm not here to get my money back. I cancelled the card and they've reimbursed what you charged. I'm not out much, just a few bucks. I just want to know why."

The flummoxed woman looked up at me and crinkled her face. "What? You want to know why?"

"Yes. Just tell me the truth. I need to know why you stole my money."

"But first," added Austin, "what's your name?"

Clearly, she didn't like this game one bit. Reluctantly, she responded. "Kathy."

"Didn't you tell me it was Mindy?" I asked.

"I don't know. I use a lot of names."

"Is it really Kathy?"

She sighed loudly. "Yes. It's really Kathy."

"Kathy what?"

After a brief pause, she answered, "Spink."

"That sounds made up." Austin folded his arms and glowered down at her.

She returned his visage with venom in her hazel eyes. "It's not!"

"Okay. Hi, Kathy Spink. He's Austin Ridenour and I'm Jay Naylor, though you probably know my name from my credit card. Now, tell me why you stole my money. And I want the truth, Kathy. It might keep you out of jail."

I could practically see her heart sink in her chest and she plopped down onto the curb. Before I could say anything else, she began to sob. "I'm sorry. I'm sorry I took your money. I've...I've had to do some horrible things. I've been...down on my luck. I had to leave Mac. He...did some...bad..." Her crying became more pronounced, drowning out the rest.

Well, I can't say I expected this reaction. Unsure of my next move, I sat on the curb next to her and gently rested my hand on the top of her head. Unexpectedly, she threw her face into the crick of my shoulder, bawling a rainstorm onto my shirt. Between sobs, she did her best to explain her situation.

From what I gathered, she moved here from her parents' house in Florida with a man she barely knew. Being young and impressionable, she took to the charming rogue, who whisked her away to Nashville. "Mac wanted to be a country music star," she said softly, once she regained her composure. "I didn't know anyone here. I left my family in Sarasota. They all warned me not to do it. But I was barely twenty-one at the time, so naïve. At first, it was great. But he quickly turned mean, especially when things didn't go his way in the music business. When he started hitting me..."

When she paused, her eyes misted over again. Looking like the waterworks might resume, I helped her to her feet as I motioned to Austin, then pointed across the street. "Hey, anyone hungry? Let's walk over to Lenny's. I could use an omelet. My treat."

As we walked, she continued. "A few months ago, after a really bad night, I told him I was leaving him. He got so mad, I really thought he might kill me. But instead, he packed up all our stuff, cancelled the lease on the apartment and left that night, in our truck. He even took my clothes. I literally had nothing but what I was wearing."

We entered Lenny's restaurant looking the motley bunch. Kathy's face was streaked with tears, her eyes puffy and red, and my shirt had a nearly perfect impression of her face on my chest. A watercolor painted with tears. As for Austin, well, he needed to stop wearing his antique ripped and faded concert jerseys. He'd had that Dio shirt for several years now, purchased at a show we went to at Pine Knob in Detroit. The hostess's eyes expanded when she caught sight of us. Clearly, she wanted to say something, but she showed tact by keeping it to herself.

Our meals ordered, Kathy looked over at me and tried to smile. "I must be quite a sight. I'm gonna use the bathroom." Austin's glare intensified, so she added, "If you don't mind."

Austin continued his harsh stare. "What do you take us for? You're gonna run off, aren't ya? Climb out the bathroom window and run away, to scam another day."

Choking back more tears, she responded, "No. I promise I won't."

"It's fine, Kathy. Go ahead. Besides Austin, she has dinner coming. She'd be daft to skip out on a free meal." I smiled at her, and she attempted one of her own. She pulled herself up and ambled toward the restroom.

"Dude," Austin said with a shake of his head, "she's not coming back."

"I don't agree. But either way, at least I confronted her."

I'd like to say I wasn't surprised when she pushed open the door and strolled back to our table, but Austin had planted the doubt in my head.

Once she sat down and took a long drink of water, she reluctantly continued. "Anyway, I've been on my own for a while now. It's been rough. I've been mostly living in the homeless woman's shelter on Cassidy Street."

Austin continued playing bad cop. "So, you make ends meet by stealing from tourists?"

"I've only done that a couple of times. Sometimes, when I get desperate, I do things... I later regret. Look, I know it's horrible what I did... what I've had to do. Believe me, I've done far worse things than steal a few bucks from you. It eats me up inside."

"No jobs in Nashville, huh?"

"It's not like I haven't tried. I just don't have the right skills. There are too many people in this town, fighting for too few jobs. I couldn't even get this lousy dump to hire me."

As luck would have it, the waitress brought our food at that moment. She eyeballed Kathy the whole time she dropped our plates in front of us. I made a mental note to give the lady a big tip.

We ate in relative silence. As we finished up our meal, I felt compelled to ask, "So Kathy, why haven't you simply gone back to Florida? It's not all that far away. Just a few-hour bus trip."

She shook her head slowly. "I kinda left things on bad terms with the folks. I don't think they'd want me back. I...we had some issues."

"Have you even talked to them?" Austin inquired.

"Not since before Mac split."

"You really should call them." I know it wasn't any of my business, but I felt for her. "Time heals. I'll bet they're worried."

She sat there silently for a moment, clearly in deep thought, before she bolted up from the booth. "Okay guys, thanks for the meal, and really, thanks for not having me arrested. Now you know my story, but I gotta go. If I don't get to the shelter soon, all the beds will be taken."

As she turned to leave, I said, "Hey, uh, you can stay with us." When she furrowed her brow I quickly added, "Not like that. I mean, there's plenty of room at the hotel. We can get you a rollaway bed."

"That's sweet, but no."

As she moved from earshot, I practically yelled, "We're at the Vacation Inn, room 211, if you, uh..."

Several people turned to ogle in my direction, igniting my blush reflex. However, Kathy did not turn around and just like that, she vanished.

Austin shrugged as he ate the last bite of his butter-slathered baked potato. "Well, there ya go. Now you know."

"Yeah," I replied with a sigh. Unfortunately, knowing didn't make me feel any better.

SIXTEEN

Without a doubt, we both had a better night's sleep than we did our last time in Nashville. That time, in that fetid little room at Bob's Snoozers Motel, the baying of the cockroaches kept us up. Not this time, no sir. We slept like babies. Well, Austin slept like a baby walrus, if that walrus had its own chainsaw. And truth be told, I slept like a baby in the sense that I fidgeted around a lot and woke up every hour. I just couldn't stop thinking about the day's events. Every time I dozed off, I saw Kathy's face. One time, I dreamt of her sleeping in a Dumpster, on a pile of broken records. Another dream had her running from some guy, her boyfriend I'd guess, while he tossed CDs at her like ninja stars. Though a weird night, I still felt a lot more comfortable sprawled on a comfy, plush bed.

I awoke to the sound of Austin singing in the shower. At least, I assumed the noises emanating from the bathroom were his version of melody. But really, I had to wonder, who sings Black Sabbath tunes while showering?

After being serenaded by a rough version of *Paranoid*, he vacated the shower amidst a plume of steam. Grinning a grin of the clean and well rested, he gestured toward the open bathroom. "All yours, buddy."

"Cool." Something always grossed me out about using a shower immediately after someone else, especially my hairy friend. But since I felt a strong urge to be squeaky clean, I sucked it up and climbed in.

Upon entering the wet shower, a comment from some old sitcom crossed my mind. "Think about the last place I wash, and the first place you wash." This made me shiver involuntarily. Fortunately, hotels plan for this sort of circumstance, so I unwrapped a fresh bar of soap and got down to it. To return the auditory favor, so to speak, I started belting out my own oddly inappropriate shower tune. At the top of my lungs, I gave him the truncated version of the Pink Floyd song *Dogs*.

Our showers completed, we hit the road fairly early.

With Austin at the wheel for this leg of the journey, we found a Mickey D's, grabbed some McMuffins, and headed onward to Florida. As Austin swallowed the last bite of his hash browns, he grinned. "Ah. The breakfast of champions. So, it won't be long now, huh?"

"Not long, no." I examined the atlas and located Bradenton, Florida. A beachfront city on the west side of the state, it looked like an easy jaunt. Then I noticed something else. "Huh," I said softly.

"What?" Austin inquired.

"According to this, Sarasota butts up to Bradenton. In fact, they apparently share an airport."

"So?"

"Kathy's family lives in Sarasota." If I'd have known how close the two cities were, I could've offered her a ride. Oh well, she wouldn't have accepted it anyway.

"Hmmph. Fascinating. So, where's the guy with the Crazy Climber cabinet at?"

"Off of Seventy-Third Street. Won't be tough to find."

Nope, not tough at all. They number their streets in Bradenton, so it made finding the place a breeze. We got to the guy's shop in the early afternoon, picked up the cabinet and monitor and loaded them up in the back of the pickup. I stood on the bed of Ol' Red, staring at my new home for Crazy. "Sure is a nice cabinet, huh?"

"Yup, it's pristine. Full size, no gouges or scratches. Even the marquee is clean. It looks a hundred times better than the old one."

That made me chuckle. "It looks a bit better than the old one used to look, but yes, a hundred times better than the one that hit the pavement and shattered into kindling."

"Uh yes, that's exactly what I meant, Mr. Obvious." He rolled his eyes at me.

"All right, buddy," I said with a grin, "I guess we hit the road."

Looking at me with obvious disdain, he replied, "Dude, look around you. We're in Florida, like two miles from the beach, in late June. It's gotta be at least eighty degrees out here. Perfect beach weather. You don't need to be back in Lansing for a few days, so let's go get our sun on! That was one of your selling points, remember?"

"But, uh, I didn't bring my swimsuit."

Austin shook his head, clearly disgusted. "Man, and I thought I was the ubergeek here. Ya see that thing over there?" Pointing at a small clothing store, he continued, "My guess is that they sell shorts and, gasp, maybe even swimming trunks. We're going over there, buying some appropriate apparel, and hitting the beach. And that's that. We came all this way, and I'm swimming in the Gulf and seeing me some bikini-clad babes."

I really couldn't fault his logic. So, we did exactly that, and within a half-hour, we were strolling along the hot, blonde-colored sand of Bradenton Beach. Being the paranoid type, I spent a majority of my time slathering sunscreen onto my alabaster-shaded neck, legs and torso. Austin, for his part, spent a good share of the day swimming. Until this moment, it hadn't occurred to me that in all the years I'd known him, I'd never seen him swim. Or strangely enough, wear shorts. His body must've had an odd temperature range, because even though he wore a light windbreaker as a winter coat, he wore long pants all summer long. Austin Ridenour, an enigma wrapped in fur, I guess.

My buddy swam in the Gulf for hours. While I can't say I appreciated seeing his body hair matted to his pallid skin like a drowned albino gorilla, Lord have mercy, he sure looked to be enjoying himself. He swam surprisingly gracefully, jumping around in the surf like a hairy dolphin.

As for me, I sat on a newly purchased towel, protecting my delicate buttocks from the sizzling sand. The stiff breeze streaming off the Gulf whipped my dishwater blonde hair around in a frenzy. I also found myself enjoying the scenery, watching the waves crashing gently against the beach. The seagulls gave me great amusement, as they darted around the vibrantly blue, nearly cloudless sky. When they settled on the beach, they'd trot toward the receding water, only to scamper back up the beach when the tide would inevitably push inland.

Oh, and of course by scenery, I also meant the many bikini-clad women as they strolled past. They mostly refrained from chuckling at my pale skin and, for a while, I imagined the smiles they tossed my way to be genuine.

But for some reason, I couldn't stop thinking about Kathy. It just didn't seem fair to me, a woman too proud to ask for assistance when that help might be so easily within reach.

A thought struck me, and I hopped up, dashing toward the bathroom area. I didn't sprint out of urgency so much, but rather out of pain from the blistering sand on my tender, bare feet. Once my gaze fell upon the pay phone, and the phone book attached by a long, metal cord, I smiled. It didn't take me long to find the section for the last name of Spink in Sarasota. Being such an odd name, I luckily only found three Spinks listed. I picked the first one, a Brad and Martha Spink, and dialed.

After a curt greeting by a female voice, I turned my head and cleared my throat before putting the receiver back to my mouth. "Hi, would you happen to have a daughter named Kathy Spink? She'd be in her mid-twenties, around five-foot tall."

The woman on the other end hesitated before replying. "Hold on."

Within moments, a gruff-sounding man came on the line. "Who is this?"

"Oh uh, my name is Jay. I met a woman in Nashville named Kathy Spink. I'm trying to locate her family."

"Why? Is everything okay?"

"Oh yeah, she's fine. Well, not fine exactly, but she's healthy. She's kinda in trouble, however, and she's too proud to ask for help."

The man's voice remained gruff and insistent. "Who is this again? Are you that guy she left with?"

"No sir, I'm no one. I just met her yesterday, and felt compelled to call you. That guy she left with, he abandoned her a few months back. He took everything. She's living in a homeless shelter, begging and stealing to survive. Look, I don't know how things went down between you, and it's certainly none of my business. I just felt like you should know that your daughter needs you. That's all."

The pause stretched on long enough for me to consider hanging up. In fact, I started moving the handset toward the cradle before I heard the man speak in a softer, more compassionate tone. "You're saying our Kathy...is in a homeless shelter?"

"Yes, sir. According to her, she's been there for the last few months."

"Say listen, Jay, is it? Where are you right now?"

"Me? I'm in Bradenton, on a pay phone at the beach."

"Which beach?"

"Oh, uh, Bradenton Beach."

"I'm familiar with it. There's a restaurant nearby called Bonnie's Beachhouse. Would you be willing to meet us there for dinner at six?"

"Yes, yes I would."

I hung up and sprinted back to my place on the beach. Not too long after I resumed my seat, Austin strolled out of the water. He walked up to me, picked up his towel and rubbed himself briefly before plopping down next to me. "Oh man, that was fantastic! You really need to go out there. It's so much fun!"

Not being much of a swimmer, I shrugged at him. "I'm good. I'm enjoying the breeze. Oh, and we have reservations for dinner."

He shot me a queer expression. "Reservations? We eating somewhere fancy?"

"I have no idea, but we're meeting a couple of people at Bonnie's Beachhouse." The idea of eating at a place that shared my ex-girlfriend's name made me cringe.

Austin felt similarly. "Ew. Betcha the food tastes bitchy and condescending." He paused to laugh before continuing. "So, who are we meeting? Did you score us a couple of ladies? Huh huh?"

"You'll see."

"Man," Austin said while applying Aloe Vera to his pink, sunburned skin, "I don't like this one bit."

"Yeah, well, I told ya to put on sunscreen."

He glared at me. "No, not that. Why did you call her parents? And more importantly, why are we meeting them?"

"I'm sure they want to hear more about their daughter."

As I finished my sentence, an older couple walked in. The man, dressed a little too formally for Florida, wore a pristine white, button-down shirt, a red-striped tie and beige dress pants. His face, like so many down here, had the look of wrinkled leather. But it went well with his thin, mostly gray hair and completely gray mustache. The lady, resplendent in a mauve, full-length cotton dress, had an air of distinction with her expensive-looking jewelry, thick, curly brown hair and faint wrinkles. I waved in their direction, and they briskly walked over.

"Are you Jay?" the gentleman asked.

"Yes, sir. And this is my friend Austin."

I offered my hand and he shook it with a firm grip. "I'm Brad, and this is my wife Martha."

Wasting no time, Martha spouted, "You've seen Kathy recently? How is she?"

I smiled nervously. "All things considered, she's okay. She's skinny but healthy."

"Thank God," Brad replied. "We haven't heard from her in nearly two years."

"Two years? She made it sound to me like she'd spoken to you in the past few months."

Martha let a sigh slip out. "Oh no, the day she left was the last contact we had with her. It broke my heart."

"That bastard took her from us," Brad said with fire in his eyes. "We could tell from the start that he was nothing but trouble. A druggie loser with visions of grandeur. He actually thought his mediocre karaoke voice could get him into the Grand Olde Opry. And that naïve daughter of ours fell for it."

"He introduced her to all sorts of bad stuff." Martha bowed her head, staring down at the table.

"So Jay," Brad asked, "How do you know her?"

I thought about lying, but why bother. "Honestly sir, she stole my wallet. We were on our way from Lansing, Michigan to California, to pick up a video game – long story. On the way down here, to pick up another video game, I tracked her down and confronted her. That's how I got her story."

Brad's eyes narrowed. "Oh, I get it. You're here to extract money from us, aren't you? Well, forget it, bub. We're through bailing her out."

I blushed involuntarily. "No no sir, you've got it all wrong. It's not about the money. She's... she's just a sweet, desperate girl who's too proud to ask you guys for help. It's none of my business, honestly, but I just couldn't let this go without contacting you. Not in good conscience." I stood up, and Austin followed suit. "I don't want anything from you. I just wanted you two to have this information. She's at a woman's shelter in Nashville, on...uh..."

"Cassidy Street," Austin said during my pause. That guy's got a mind like a steel trap!

"Yeah, Cassidy Street. We've taken up too much of your time. Good day."

"Wait!" screamed Martha. She turned to her husband, and after a few moments of hushed conversation, she turned back to us. "So, when are you boys headed back to Michigan?"

"Oh, probably tomorrow."

"And how much did our daughter steal from you?"

"Geez... I had around ninety dollars in cash and she charged a couple hundred before I cancelled my card. But Visa said they'd remove the charges, so I'm really not worried about it."

In one swift motion, Brad pulled out his wallet and handed me two one hundred-dollar bills.

"Oh sir," I said with my palms in the air, "I truly don't want your money. That's not what this is about."

Brad's face curled into a surprisingly heart-warming smile. "I know, son. So, how about if you earn your money back? If you would, please take this money, buy a bus ticket from Nashville to Sarasota, and give it to our daughter. You can keep the change. It should be more than enough. We'd go ourselves, but

I'm in the middle of an important business negotiation, at a crucial stage. I can't afford to be gone now. And I wouldn't let Martha travel there on her own. So, will you help us?"

I hesitated, but eventually accepted the cash. "You have to understand, I really can't be sure we'll be able to find her. But if we do, I promise you I'll do as you've requested. But if I can't locate her, give me your address and I'll see to it your money is returned."

"You'll find her. I just know you will." Martha stood up and embraced me with a powerful, motherly hug. "Bless you, boys! Find our Kathy. Make sure she knows she's welcome."

"Tell her all is forgiven." Brad's warm smile added realism to his words.

Before either of us realized it, Martha gripped Austin in a hug as well. He fought hard to suppress it, but a hushed shriek escaped his pursed lips as the pain of his tender sunburn overwhelmed his senses. A tear popped out and ran down his cheek. "Oh, you're moved to emotion, too," Martha said as a tear of her own came trickling down.

"Emotion," he squeaked, "right."

As we left the restaurant, I had an odd feeling rolling around inside of me. Though I hated to admit it, some part of me wanted to pocket the money and hit the highway for home. After all, they'd never know and I doubt I'd ever see any of these people again. Besides, I certainly didn't owe that little thief a thing. In fact, she spent my money...on frivolous stuff like food and clothing.

Okay, my mind didn't need to go there to assure I would do the right thing. Although it might have been out of character for me to track her down and confront her, not to mention locating her parents, but I've always had a strong sense of right and wrong. Like it or not, I accepted this mission and I had to see it through, or at least give it my best shot.

I had my hands positioned on the wheel to make a left turn when I heard Austin squeal next to me. Assuming I made the seatbelt dig into his pink flesh, I uttered, "Oh sorry man, did I stop too fast for ya?"

Instead, he pointed over to the right. "Look, an arcade!"

Sure enough, a large, single-story building called Pirates Cove beckoned to us. Quickly, I shot from the left lane to the right, causing a couple of cars to blare their horns loudly at my brashness.

As we pulled in to the parking lot of Pirates Cove, a large paper banner caught our attention.

Arcade Contest Today! Top Prize – five hundred dollars!

"Well!" Austin rubbed his hands together greedily. "I know what we're doing today."

SEVENTEEN

Pirates Cove reminded us of some of the great arcades of our youth. We had a couple of fantastically large, dimly-lit video arcades in East Lansing, both named Pinball Pete's. They had it all: twenty-five cent Cokes, dozens of the best state-of-the-art arcade games and pinball machines of the era, and no matter what time of day we went there, we'd always run into at least one buddy or classmate. Pete's was where I played Tempest, Galaga and countless other games for the first time. Back then, everything only cost a quarter.

As we strolled around the Cove, we saw all sorts of wonderful games from times past: Sinistar, 1941, and yes, even good old Galaga. Austin elbowed me as he spotted a game dear to our hearts. "Well well well, would ya look at that."

Did my eyes deceive me? Hell no! I stood in an actual arcade with an actual Crazy Climber. I couldn't recall the last time I saw one in the wild. "Oh, we'll be playing that later, no matter what!"

Walking up to the makeshift card table, we said hello to the man taking registration for the big event. The skinny guy with his long, scraggily hair emanating around a decent-sized bald circle – we often referred to it as the Ben Franklin look – waved and returned our greeting. "So," Austin said to Ben, "give us the lowdown on this contest."

"Sure thing, fellas." The guy had a slight lisp, and knowing Austin, he had to fight the urge to giggle as much as I did. "This contest will be three rounds. First round, contestants will be playing Zoo Keeper. Top ten scorers go on to round two. Then, contestants play Galaga." I glanced over at Austin, his big grin mirroring my own. "Top three play the final round. That game will be…"

Internally, my mind chanted, "Say Crazy Climber, please say Crazy Climber."

"…Donkey Kong."

I think he could hear both our hearts drop, but if so, he paid it no mind. "Twenty dollar entry fee."

We both plopped our money on the table.

The contest didn't begin for a couple of hours, so we took turns, along with some other contestants, playing Zoo Keeper and Donkey Kong. It had been a while for both of us, so we used our turns to wisely refresh ourselves with the playing of these games. We saw no point in brushing up on Galaga.

When the time came, we felt as ready as possible. Our competition ranged from teenagers who weren't even alive when some of these games debuted, to men old enough to be our fathers. Frankly, the sheer number of contestants shocked us. There had to be close to forty males here, and not too surprisingly, only a couple of women in the bunch. Apparently doing the math in his head, Austin whispered to me, "They easily made enough money on entry fees to pay the top prize." That revelation pleased me. After all, arcades had started a downward slide in recent years, but thanks to events like this, they could still have their moments.

As the contest began, Ben walked up to each contestant and handed out a sheet of paper with a number printed on it. "Wear these around your necks. I will call you by your number."

I showed mine to Austin. "Sweet. I'm eleven. My favorite number."

"Good for you." He showed me his twenty-four as he whispered, "These things make me feel like we're about to run in a geek marathon."

At that point, Ben flipped on the tripod-mounted camera, and the giant projection screen in the center of the room flickered to life. This way, we could all watch the game player's progress on the big screen.

They took us in numerical order, so my turn on Zoo Keeper came up fairly quickly. At that point, the scores ranged from mediocre to fantastic and everywhere in-between. I exhaled loudly and, with all eyes upon me, I stepped up to the machine.

Fortunately, I found Zoo Keeper to be a fairly straightforward game. In the first two rounds, I ran Zoo Keeper Zeke around the rectangular play field, adding fresh layers of bricks to keep the animals from escaping, collecting power-ups and grabbing the net to catch any escaped critters. The problem for me occurred in the third level, where the game format changed to become a platform-jumping game, trying to hop to the top of a series of tiny, constantly moving ledges. This round came up every third level, and every third level would cost me a life or two.

I played steadily for a few minutes, surviving six rounds. Finishing with a score of 84,600, I now ranked third.

With my first round completed, I stood back and watched my opponents play.

When it became contestant number twenty-four's turn, I found myself in fifth place. Apparently, I had a pretty decent score after all. Austin grinned at me as he stepped up to give it a go. Knowing the types of games Austin liked, I assumed he hadn't played Zoo Keeper much. However, he smoked my score and still had one life left. By the time his last Zeke died, he sat with 149,900, the highest score so far.

As he sauntered by me, I high-fived him. "Dang, dude! Fantastic score. You're all but guaranteed to make the second round."

He showed me a smug grin. "I know." Then he added, "Y'know, apart from today, I had never played the game before."

"Huh." Oh well, he'll probably win this whole thing, but at least it'll be in the family, so to speak.

When the last guy came to take his turn, I sat on the cusp of elimination as the tenth-highest score. This dude, a tow-headed teen with more pimples than skin, looked like a typical gaming geek. However, I held on to the hope he was more of a modern day gamer. I'll bet he spent his days playing Doom II on the Playstation or Quake II on the PC, or whatever online fragfest the kids played nowadays.

Pimple-boy played like his life depended on it, and he fought hard, wiggling his body around like he had insects crawling on his skin. But in the end, he finished with a couple hundred points less than I did. I had made it to the next round.

As I passed by an old guy with thick, white hair bound tightly in a long ponytail, he said to me, "Hey, ya snuck in. Me too, I'm Manny, a.k.a. number nine."

"Cool. I'm Jay, pleased to meet ya."

We shook hands firmly. "Likewise. So, what'cha gonna do with the money, if ya win?"

Shrugging, I said, "Oh I dunno. Haven't really thought about it. Honestly, I don't expect to win. If anyone here's gonna win, it's my buddy over there."

He momentarily turned his attention to Austin. "What, lobster boy?" I chuckled at the reference to his still-apparent sunburn. "All ya gotta do to beat him is smack him on the back once or twice. The pain'll knock him out for sure."

After we both finished laughing, I said, "I'll keep that as a last resort. So what about you? If you win, I mean."

"Probably get me a new kidney. Either that or a car."

"Can ya get a kidney for five hundred?"

"Used. Same for the car."

"Of course, ya can't beat that new kidney smell."

"True," he replied, "but I'm on a budget. All right buddy, good luck to ya."

"Same to you," I yelled as he merged with the throng of people.

Once the second round began, the crowd had grown exponentially. Even though few of them were playing the games, they all had a hot dog or a pop in their hands. Not a bad marketing angle for the owner of this place.

I sidled up to Austin. "All right buddy, our game's up next." I reared my arm back to give him a violent open-handed slap on the back, but I decided against such extremes.

"This oughta be fun," he replied with a broad smile.

Since Austin had the highest score, they had him go first on Galaga. Oh man, did he kick butt! He could regularly top 300,000 without an issue, but I had never, in all our years playing, seen him top 500,000. He finished with the astronomical score of 573,120. When he lost the last life, everybody stood in silent awe for a moment, before the cheers erupted. The other players, myself included, knew we had our work cut out for us.

I had the distinct advantage of going last, so I got to watch all the other players fumble for that massive high score. I think it proved to be a mental issue, and it cost many of them dearly. The scores ranged from under 100,000 to a shade over 300,000.

When my turn came up, I had to beat 302,300 to get third, or 482,060 to get second. I had never seen 400,000, and 300,000 came very rarely for me, so I knew I had to have the game of my life.

Normally, my strategy was simply to kill, kill and kill some more. I would usually just clear out a screen as quickly as possible and go on to the next level. But I paid special attention to how the top three played their games. They all worked to maximize points, by leaving groups at the top and not shooting until the enemy advanced. It proved to be effective, but it led to a more stressful game than usual. Sweat poured down my face like tiny rivers and my heart throbbed in my chest as if I was on mile five of a foot race. Earlier, I had laughed at some of the others who twisted and flailed their bodies while they played, but heck, I found myself doing the exact same thing. It probably looked hilarious, but it proved surprisingly effective. Confidence slowly rose inside of me.

By relying on my newly-realized strategy, I managed to cruise to my all-time best score of 336,810. That meant I made it to the final round.

Apart from Austin, my other opponent was none other than Manny. He congratulated me with another handshake and Austin with a firm slap to his back. Austin winced in agony, while Manny flashed me a wink. "Oh, sorry bro, didn't notice the sunburn."

Since the final round didn't start for about an hour, the three of us grabbed a bite to eat at Bonnie's. We told Manny all about our adventures thus far, and he sounded impressed. "All that for a video game. You boys went through a lot, to be sure. But really, ya need to do this kinda stuff while you're still young. Take me, for instance. I'm almost sixty now, but I still make a point of embracing my youth whenever possible. I exercise every day, be it jogging on the beach or playing volleyball with the kids. It keeps me agile and vibrant. Why, two weeks ago, I bungee jumped for the first time. Later this year, I plan on jumping out of an airplane."

"You're gonna take a parachute, right?" Austin asked as he popped a fry into his mouth.

He winked as he replied, "Perhaps. Haven't decided yet."

"So Manny," I had to ask, "how come you're so good at these video games?"

"Why, I come to Pirates Cove nearly every day. I have to; I work here. I run the mini-golf course, and when I'm not working or playing pool or SkeeBall, I play video games. I get all my games free. Kinda makes up for the lousy pay, I reckon."

Austin's smile evaporated. "I dunno, old man. Kinda sounds like a conflict of interest to me. Don't they usually have an 'employees not eligible' disclaimer for these types of contests?"

"Another way for the owner to make up for lousy pay." When he saw the serious expression on our faces, he held up his finger. "Tell ya what, boys. If you don't make a stink about this, I'll do something for you to level the playing field."

"Like what?" Austin inquired.

"Oh, you'll see. Trust me on this."

EIGHTEEN

As the final round began, the Ben Franklin looking dude walked up to the podium and cleared his throat. "To all of you, and especially to the three finalists, I have an announcement to make. Unfortunately, the Donkey Kong machine has malfunctioned, so the final round will be played on Crazy Climber."

First, I looked at Austin, who sported a gigantic grin. He never much cared for Donkey Kong. Then, I turned to Manny. The old man smiled and winked at me. Oh, I understood now. He did this in an attempt to repay us for not ratting him out. Of course, he had probably logged as many hours on Crazy as he had on any other machine in this arcade, but he probably figured it would give us a fighting chance.

Ironically, it didn't do me any favors. Throughout this whole adventure, I had only played Crazy once, and I sucked badly. But still, I had to appreciate his gift to us.

We drew numbers from a baseball cap to ascertain our playing order, with Manny picking number one. Playing like a man who had enjoyed Crazy many times in his life, he didn't lose his first life until the second building. By the time the fourth building took his final life, he had compiled a respectable score of 150,430.

Next, Austin moseyed up to the game, looking quite confident. I already knew he could make it at least that far, having seen him do it during our journey. However, he lost his rhythm fairly early on, losing a life on the first building. The gasp from the crowd made me laugh. They were clearly getting into this contest. Austin saw the third building, but had only the one Climber left. He died before the helicopter could airlift him from the rooftop. That meant Manny had the lead, and only I stood between him and a new used kidney, or a car.

I had hoped I wouldn't be nervous, but oh no, my palms felt damp and clammy, sweat oozed off my forehead, and I swear everyone could see me shaking. Before I stepped up to the plate, Austin did his best to comfort me. Dropping his arm across my shoulder, he turned his head to look me in the eye. "Dude," he said with no discernible emotion, "Don't worry about this shot. If you miss it, we lose." Oh lovely, he's paraphrasing our favorite movie, *Caddyshack*. Actually, it helped a bit in easing my tension, and I cracked a smile. He then gave me a quick slap on the back. "Seriously, ya got this, dude. Have fun with it."

I panned the crowd, seeing the hopeful faces. One guy yelled, with a pronounced Mexican accent, "You can do eet!" I think that quote came from yet another movie, but I couldn't recall which one. Manny even tossed me a smile and two thumbs-up. Okay, time to do this thing.

Turning my back on the crowd, I pushed the button and started the game. I decided to follow Austin's advice, and have fun. *Just put one arm in front of the other. Make the Crazy Climber climb the building, one window at a time. I still can't believe he doesn't have a name. How queer. I think I'll call you Eduardo.* That made me smile, and I used my mirth to enjoy the climb.

My heart playing a wicked Neil Peart drum solo in my chest, I pushed Eduardo up the building swiftly, reaching the top of building number one with all lives intact.

The second building got me almost instantly. Darn those tumbling girders! But I kept going, and managed to circumvent any other issues as I completed building two.

Though I had seen several others play building three, I had never made it that far. However, I decided to call that a strength, having no preconceived notions. Calling upon what I saw Manny and Austin do, and using my instincts, I got about halfway up before losing my second life. The crowd yelled, "Awww," in unison. I only had one guy left now.

Fighting hard, I made it past the final obstacle on building three, grabbed the waiting chopper, and proceeded to building four. When I took my hands off the joysticks, they started shaking violently. I quickly reaffirmed my grasp on the sticks, with a death grip that rapidly turned my knuckles white. Realizing I still had a lot of points to go, I whispered, "Don't lose focus, Jay." Then I practically yelled, "Go, Eduardo!

Randy D Pearson

You can do eet!" This caused some puzzled laughter from the crowd.

I continued to play with all my heart and reflexes, reaching the spot where Manny lost his last life. Recalling how he died, I zagged when he zigged, and the obstacle missed me. My Eduardo didn't last long after that, but my score ended at 150,550. Holy crap, I won!

The hoopla surrounding my win surprised me. I mean, sure, the crowd had really gotten into it, so their adulation seemed appropriate enough. But the camera crew, which I hadn't even noticed until now, caught me off guard. Must've been a slow news day. A reporter, with the blackest, most amazingly wind-resistant-looking hair I had ever seen, approached me. "Dirk Irtly, channel forty-two action news central. So, what are you going to do with the money?"

I gave him an exaggerated shrug. "Well Dirk, who knows. Perhaps I'll buy me some nice hair like yours. Is that real Teflon?" I reached up to feign touching it, and he twitched. Then he glared at me like I dropped a deuce in his Whisky Sour. "Kidding. It'll help me get home to Michigan."

That perked him up, so I had to waste a few minutes explaining the journey thus far. I found myself enjoying the attention, until he asked one of those stupid interview questions. "You must really like video games."

I couldn't help myself. "Zounds, no! Are you kidding me? It's a horrible addiction. If my sponsor knew I was here playing these video games, he'd kick me outta Gamer's Anonymous. Man, it's like Crank, but with a chance at better teeth." I gave him my toothiest grin. It threw him so far off balance, I felt the need to give him something at least semi-honest. "No, but really, I'm not normally all that good at video games, but I

182

guess I had the perfect combination of luck and, well, more luck."

"I see. What game did you come down to Florida to pick up?"

"Ironically enough, it was Crazy Climber."

"Why is that ironic?"

"Seriously?" I asked while tossing a thumb at the machine, in the shot behind us. "I won on Crazy Climber. I'm here picking up Crazy Climber. Zing!"

Wait for it…"Oh! Well yes, that is ironic. What are the odds?"

From behind me, Austin yelled, "44,792 to one!" as he strolled through the camera shot with a wave and a smile.

"Math geek," I said casually. "Oh, did I tell ya I'm recently recovering from hip surgery?"

"Wow, that's amazing. How did you break it?"

"Oh no, I didn't break anything. I just didn't feel I was hip enough."

Austin, from just off camera, chimed in with, "Bah-dah-bum, chee!" A classic rimshot noise if ever I heard one. "But seriously folks."

"So hey," I said, "when will this air?"

Mumbling under his breath, the flummoxed reporter replied, "Never, if I have anything to say about it."

"Well, good luck with that." I said as he lowered the microphone and walked off. "But seriously, great hair, man! Where can I buy me some hair like that? Is it shellac or more of an oil-based lacquer? Is it commercial grade or can any schmuck get some? Hello? Hey, get back here!"

NINETEEN

The scraggly-haired owner, whom I'd mentally named Ben Franklin, handed me the giant novelty five-hundred dollar check, and I donned a smile through the seemingly endless array of photos and video cameras. Once the hoopla died down, I turned and shook the man's hand. "This is cool, thanks, uh..."

Recognizing the reason for my pause, he answered my non-verbalized question. "I'm Ben. Ben Watkins."

Before my mind could stop my mouth, I asked, "Really?"

"Uh, yeah. Why?"

"Nothing. So hey, where can I cash a check this big? Is there a giant bank around here?"

He chuckled as he replied, "Nah, that's just a prop. In fact, I need that back, for next time. I'll get ya the cash. Follow me."

Austin and I did as instructed, following him back to his office and storeroom. As I stood next to Ben, Austin wandered a few feet away. After a moment, I heard him yell, "Hey, are these games dead?"

With cash in hand, I followed the owner into his storeroom. Austin stood wide-eyed in front of a couple of arcade games. One, Virtua Fighter, had the back opened up with its guts hanging out. The Tempest machine still had its cabinet shut. "Virtua Fighter has seen better days, but Tempest is fine. I just don't have the room anymore. All these new multi-player racing games with the built-in seats, the Dance Dance games with the huge pads and all that, they take up so much real estate. I had to start moving some of the old games out." He paused and released a small sigh. "Man, I miss the simple old days. I say gimme a game with a joystick or a knob and I'm happy."

Austin felt the need to interject. "My knob makes me happy, I'll tell ya what."

After I elbowed him, I asked, "So, you gonna sell Tempest?"

"Maybe. Why, ya interested?"

"Maybe."

His eyes darted from my face, to the cash in my hand, and back to me in a split-second. "Five hundred?"

This made me laugh out loud. Nice thought, a straight-up trade. But I figured I could work him. "I did some research before we left Michigan. How about three-fifty?" Other than the few I stumbled across on eBay, I really hadn't done any such research, and I would've gladly paid it all for the game. But heck, why not try to haggle?

He eyeballed me for a moment. "Four hundred."

Counting out and pocketing a hundred, I handed him the rest. "Sold!"

As we wheeled the game to the truck with his dolly, which I thanked him profusely for allowing us to use, Austin felt compelled to ask me, "What made you decide to buy this?"

"For one, I love Tempest. It's my second favorite game, or maybe third after Crazy and Galaga." I lowered my voice. "And for two, Four hundred? Dude, that's a steal. They sell for a lot more than that online. Besides, it's free money. It's like I won Tempest."

"Okey-doke, I can buy that logic. Sweet!"

With my prize secured in the back of Ol' Red, we drove back to our hotel room and turned in for the evening.

After a good night's sleep, Austin and I decided to get on the road. "We should hit Nashville by late morning."

Austin ran his fingers through his unkempt hair and groaned. "Are we really gonna bother? Can't we just go home? It's not like they'd ever know."

"You didn't really just say that, did you? I am not gonna incur the wrath of karma over this. We've been entrusted with this quest, and you know darn well hafta do it. Or at least we'll give it our best try."

An overly exaggerated sigh shot from Austin's mouth. "Yeah, I know. That was a test. And you passed. Yay, good for you and all that." That last bit didn't sound genuine to me.

"So what, you're now playing the part of the devil on my shoulder?"

"Never leave home without 'em." He showed me his best evil grin, mimicking devil ears with his fingers.

We pulled into Nashville at a shade past eleven o'clock, probably the textbook definition of late morning. After a bit of breakfast at another Lenny's and making certain our Crazy Climber cabinet, monitor and Tempest were secure and well hidden under the bright blue tarp, we drove to the bus station. Austin, continuing his role as shoulder-devil, tried to convince me not to buy the bus ticket. "Dude, it's entirely possible we won't be able to find her. You know this."

I mimicked flicking him off my shoulder. "Don't worry, Satan. We'll find her. Karma won't let me down this time. Besides, and I'm only telling you this to make you feel better, these things are fully refundable." They weren't, of course, but it did seem to ease his troubled mind, so he stopped nagging me after that little fib.

With ticket in hand, we headed straight to Cassidy Street, in search of the woman's shelter. We went up and down the lengthy street three times before we finally found Barb's House, a surprisingly small, unassuming brick building with lots of tiny, rectangular windows. We parked and walked inside.

The interior was bright and cheerful, with lots of pastel flowers adorning the walls. We felt many eyes upon us as we entered, and it took me a minute before I understood why. As two men entering a battered and abused center for women, the staff and patrons probably placed us as bad guys, losers looking to reclaim our property or something equally horrific. As I approached the front desk, I plastered my best smile upon my increasingly pale-feeling face. "Uh, hi. I am trying to locate a, um, customer... inmate..."

The chunky, homely administrator looked at me through old-school horn-rimmed glasses, her anger barely contained. She actually snorted before she spoke. "Do you mean guest?"

My blushing quickly overcame my previously pale complexion. "Oh yes, I'm sorry. A guest. Her name is Kathy Spink."

Glaring as she looked us up and down, she replied, "And why are you looking for this lady? Are one of you the reason she's been staying here?"

At this moment, I feared Austin would say something stupid and/or inappropriate. Fortunately for me, he wanted nothing to do with this whole situation, so he remained silent. "No ma'am," I said. "I've been in touch with her parents and they've given me something to give to her. And I have a message from them."

I tried smiling again, but she wouldn't stop with the accusatory stare. After an uncomfortably long silence, she picked up the phone and hit a few buttons. Immediately, I heard the intercom crackle to life overhead. The woman spoke calmly but forcefully. "Code Blue at the front desk." It echoed throughout the lobby, down the hall and bounced violently off the glass doors.

From behind me, I heard Austin whisper, "Oh crap."

Pure will power kept me from sprinting out the door. After all, I had done nothing wrong, even though these circumstances made me feel otherwise.

After a few more tense seconds, three men walked out from behind a large set of heavy wooden doors. Two big, burly guys in scrubs flanked the smaller man wearing a light blue button-down shirt with a red-striped tie. The well-dressed man said firmly, with the thinnest of smiles, "My name is Mark Abernathy. How can I help you gentlemen today?"

"Hello Mr. Abernathy," I said as I resumed feeling pale and light-headed. "My name is Jay Naylor. This is Austin Ridenour. There is a woman who stays here named Kathy Spink. I just returned from Florida, where I met with her parents. They gave me some money and a bus ticket, so she could go back home." I pulled out the bus ticket, holding it in the air to prove my validity. "Is she here?"

Though I felt uncomfortable with it, I let the man reach out and pluck the ticket from my grasp. He examined it thoroughly. "This is for tomorrow morning. You're apparently confident you'll find her."

"When I bought it, they told me it can be exchanged for any other day."

He replied, "Good," before handing it back to me. He then turned to the chunky lady at the counter. "Ruth, could you check to see if Kathy Spink has checked in recently?" Then he faced me once again. "You do understand why we're so cautious here, don't you?"

"Yes, you have to be careful. I understand perfectly."

"How do you know this woman? Are you friends of the family?"

Man, I had no intention of telling the truth here. "Uh, yes, friends of the family. Her parents asked me to help out. I'm doing them, and her, a favor."

We all turned when Chubby, I mean Ruth said, "No, she hasn't been here in two days."

"I'm sorry, Mr. Naylor."

Oh no! "Shoot. I wonder where she's at?"

"That is hard to say. I don't know Kathy personally – there are so many young women coming through this establishment – but a lot of them only stay here as a last resort. She might have found, if you'll pardon the vernacular, a better offer."

Austin, quiet until now said, "She's been known to steal from tourists."

My eyes narrowed to slits and I shot him a quick glare before turning back to Mr. Abernathy. "Say, if I can't find her around town, can I leave the bus ticket with your organization? Can I be sure she'll get it?"

The well-dressed man smiled, and a bit more genuinely than before. "I can't promise she'll ever come back here, of course. But if she does, you can rest assured she will receive it. Every guest must check in before they are allowed to stay. We can flag her name to show her she has mail."

As he reached out his hand, I hesitated. "Tell ya what. I'm going to check out some of her hangouts first. If I don't find her by day's end, I'll come back."

"Certainly, but please be back by six. We close the offices then."

"Jay," Austin asked, "just how long are we gonna do this?" Clearly, Austin wanted to get home.

I had to agree with his sentiment. This trip had been all kinds of interesting, but I really missed sleeping in my own bed. And as we drove around to the places where she used my credit card, as well as some local bars, the monotony grew exponentially. We even strolled into the MegaShop, but when they said we were banned from that store, they weren't kidding. We barely stepped foot on their tile floor before being escorted off the premises.

After checking every place we could think of, twice, we decided to finish our search at the bar where we first met her, Bob's Country Palace.

As we pushed open the door to Bob's, I shook my head slowly. Did that surly waitress ever take a day off? She took one look at us and broke out in laughter. "You two again? Ain't you ever gonna leave?"

"Don't we wish," Austin replied. "I want one of them tasty burgers, but no more beer. I want a rum and Coke. What're the chances?"

Austin's enquiry apparently tickled her funny bone. She snickered loudly before responding. "I'm in a better mood, so sure, why not? And what about you, Casanova?"

"Same. Say, have you seen...I know you'll say "I ain't seen nuthin'." But seriously, that woman we hung out with last time...ya seen her lately?"

She eyeballed me like I had stiffed her on a tip. "The girl that ran out the door last time she saw you? You really think I'm gonna help you?"

"I know what that must've looked like, but we had a good talk after that. She told me her story. Afterwards, I looked up her parents." Holding up the ticket, I added, "They wanted me to give her a bus ticket home."

After perusing the ticket, she whistled. "I'll be damned. So, you're a regular Good Somalian."

That made me laugh. I assumed she meant Good Samaritan. "Yeah, one of them. So, have ya seen her lately?"

"I ain't seen nuthin'." She paused, then added, "Really. But I'll keep my eyes open for her."

"Thanks, I appreciate that. If I don't find her before we leave, which will be soon, please tell her the ticket is waiting at the shelter for her. Her parents really miss her." Then, I snapped my fingers. "So, how 'bout the grub n' booze?"

"Don't get smart, boys." She grinned at us. I think we finally won her over.

We sat there, eating and drinking, for a lot longer than Austin would've liked. I just couldn't bring myself to leave. But the clock neared midnight, and she never showed. While staring at the clock, a realization struck me. "Crap! The shelter closed hours ago!"

Austin shook his head slowly, stood up, steadied himself, and staggered over to the Galaga machine. As he moseyed off, he slurred, "I guess you're gonna need to get us a room, moneybags. I'm off to play another game."

He had a point. We needed a place to stay, and I doubted the woman's shelter would let us crash there. As I sauntered toward the door, I nearly plowed in to a woman as she entered the bar.

"Oh, sorry Miss," I said as I sidled by. I nearly continued walking until I realized I recognized her long, auburn hair. "Kathy?!"

Kathy spun around with eyes wide, looking like a frightened gazelle. Then, recognition seeped into her brain. "Oh, hey. It's you," she said flatly. No enthusiasm whatsoever. "I thought you were going home."

Oh, I couldn't help but beam when she fed me that line. "We will be in the morning. And so will you." With that, I held up the bus ticket and handed it to her.

She looked at it with a clear lack of understanding. "Okay, you bought me a bus ticket to Sarasota. That's...annoyingly thoughtful, but..."

Quickly interrupting, I said, "Actually, this is from your parents. Brad and Martha miss you very much.

They forgive you and they want you to come home. They asked me to deliver it to you."

Rage bubbled up from somewhere deep within her. "Oh, they forgive me! *They* forgive *me!*" The anger in her eyes confused me. Not how I pictured this interaction going, to be sure. "Did they tell you how horribly they treated me? Don't let them fool you. They couldn't wait to get rid of me."

"Kathy, look. I didn't mean to get in the middle of all this..."

"What do you mean, you didn't mean? Of course you did! What, did they somehow find you?"

I sighed heavily. "Okay, I probably overstepped my bounds. But you seemed like you needed help. I was already in your hometown, so I looked them up. You seem miserable here and they certainly seemed just as unhappy. They asked me to give you this ticket, to tell you they were sorry for everything and to remind you that you always have a home. That's all. Sorry I bothered you."

Pushing around her, I quickly walked out into the parking lot. She may have said something, but I tuned it out and hopped into the truck.

For no particular reason, I turned left out of Bob's parking lot instead of right, and sped off down the street. Even though our Vacation Inn sat in the other direction, I felt like driving around aimlessly for a while.

During my trip, I couldn't help but replay the whole scene in my mind. My own anger surged to the surface. How dare she treat me that way! With all the trouble I went through, tracking them down, then tracking her down, what do I get for my trouble? Yelled at by an ungrateful little thief, that's what. Man, Austin was right. It doesn't pay to help anyone. Screw people!

After about twenty minutes of driving, I sped past the Vacation Inn, which startled me. While apparently paying so little attention to my surroundings, I had somehow managed to come full-circle. Slamming on the brakes, I did a U-turn and darted into the parking lot. Turned out they still had our old room vacant, so I booked 211 for one final night.

On the way back to get my partner, my mind wouldn't shut the hell up. The more I thought about it, the more my rational side kicked in. Sometimes, I hated the part of me that just had to see both sides of an issue. Okay, sure, she didn't ask for any help. Who was I to think I knew best? Here I was, trying to usurp her pride, like she couldn't make it without her mommy and daddy. I should've left well enough alone, but no, I had to butt in, like the valiant hero. Apparently, no one needed saving here.

I pulled back into the parking lot of Bob's Country Palace, hoping to waltz in, get Austin and head back to the hotel. But as I pushed open the door, a sigh forced its way out. Austin and Kathy sat together at our table, with Austin tipping his rum and Coke to the ceiling while Kathy crammed a big handful of fries into her mouth.

Ignoring her, I said to Austin, "Hey, I got us the same room at the Vacation Inn."

"211 was still available?"

"Yup. Ya ready?"

Kathy's eyes got all glassy as she looked at me. I wondered how many beers she had conned Austin out of, but when she stood up and grabbed hold of my hands, tears simultaneously escaped from both her eyes. "Oh Jay, I'm sorry. You did an amazing, generous thing, and I treated you like crap. If you would've listened to Austin, you two would already be home by now."

Grinning, Austin added, "I told her how much of a bastard I am. She knows she's lucky you don't listen to me, your shoulder Satan, very often."

Before I could utter a word, she continued. "Look, I'm not used to people doing anything nice for me, unless they want, y'know, something in return. And my parents...well, it's complicated. But I know they only want what's best for me. Despite everything, I know they love me. So, I'm going to use this ticket and go stay with them for a while, until I can get back on my feet. Besides, I've heard a rumor that my old boyfriend's back here in Nashville, and it would really suck running into that bastard again. Getting out of here is really the best move for me."

I finally allowed myself a meager smile. "I'm glad to hear that. I hope everything works out for you."

"It's gotta be better than this place." With that, she took the two steps over to me, craned her neck upwards and planted a big, wet kiss on my lips. She tasted like ketchup and beer, but I didn't mind. "Thank you, Jay. I'll never forget this."

"Me neither. Good luck."

As I watched her exit the bar, Austin elbowed me in the side. "Dude, you could totally nail her now."

I laughed at my friend's perfectly timed inappropriate comment. "You crack me up, little buddy. You've had enough rum. Let's get outta here."

Even though Austin snored louder than usual after all that rum, sounding a bit like a demon with asthma running a jackhammer, I slept a dreamless, restful sleep. When I awoke, a large, sleepy smile spread across my face as I stretched. I felt at peace and extremely well rested. "I guess this is how a man feels when he does the honorable thing," I whispered to myself. Sure, it crossed my mind to bolt with the cash, and I definitely didn't enjoy wasting a day tracking her down, but with how I felt now, I clearly did the right thing.

With Austin's suitcase and my duffel bag in our hands, we walked out to the truck to enjoy a leisurely breakfast before beginning the last leg of our journey.

As we approached Ol' Red, Austin let out a panicked gasp. I started to say, "What, is Lenny's closed?" when I glanced up at the bed of our truck. It no longer contained my Crazy Climber cabinet or the blue tarp. Tempest and the monitor were still there, right where we had left them, but not the empty cabinet. "Oh, come on!" I yelled. "Seriously?"

We knew this wasn't the best part of the city, what with homeless shelters, liquor stores and burned-out churches dotting the landscape. But really, who in their right mind would steal an empty cabinet?

After releasing a long, loud, exaggerated sigh, I looked at Austin. "Okay, lovely. So question number one is why?"

Rubbing his several-day growth of chin fur, he replied, "Well, there's no real money in it. It can't be pawnable."

"Right. And it's kinda unwieldy, so they probably didn't get all that far." Out of sheer desperation, we began walking down the street, looking into alleys and side roads. We didn't get far before we realized this method would take forever, so we hoofed it back to the truck.

Driving all over the city, we glanced down every side street and looked into any open garage or shed. This method took up a lot of time, several hours in fact, and yielded nothing.

After wasting the better part of the morning, we realized our hunger had never been satisfied, so we circled back and hit Lenny's. Perhaps a stack of pancakes would help clearer thoughts form.

Once we had our orders placed, the waiter, a young, chipper man with spiky blonde hair and a piercing centered just under his lower lip, saw the look of consternation on our faces. "Oh now, it can't be that bad. You'll feel much better after you've eaten."

Looking up at him, I replied, "I doubt it'll do much. We've had our property stolen while we slept."

"Oh. Sorry to hear that." He thought for a moment before continuing. "You stayed in the area?"

"Yeah, at the Vacation Inn."

Under different circumstances, the grimace he displayed would've made me laugh. "Ouch. Not the best part of town to spend the night in. What was stolen, if you don't mind me asking?"

"An arcade game cabinet. Just an empty cabinet," Austin said.

"And a blue tarp," I added.

"Odd things to swipe. Well, I wish ya luck, guys." With that, he left to go check on our food.

When he brought our plates a few minutes later, he said something that made us both slap our heads. "So boys, what did the police say when you reported it?"

Austin looked at me sheepishly. "Oh sure, the police. What kinda moron wouldn't call the cops right away?"

I quickly added, "Say, on an unrelated matter, can you tell us how to get to the nearest police station?"

Once we completed our meals, leaving the guy a pretty decent tip for the advice, we hopped into the truck and rolled on over to the neighborhood Nashville Police Station precinct. After waiting an annoyingly long time for our turn at the front desk, a melancholic black female acknowledged our presence. We described our situation, and she ushered us to sit around a desk in the far corner of the large, non-partitioned room. The desk, a cluttered affair, had a large piece of oak with the name Detective Falters stamped on it. We sat there for nearly a half-hour, waiting for someone to care. I turned and whispered to Austin, even though the background noise would've made it impossible for anyone to hear, "Man, this is a waste of time. I figured they'd take our info and we'd be on our way."

"We're very busy here, gentlemen," boomed a voice from behind us. We turned to see a hulking man looming over us, his size from both thick muscles and overall girth. The word *solid* would best describe him. If a hurricane hit this place right now, I would not hesitate to grab a leg. "I am Detective Falters. How can I help you gentlemen today?"

We spent a minute explaining our situation to the detective. For his part, he didn't seem amused about the situation, which I appreciated. He didn't show an over-abundance of caring, either. "While I can sympathize with your predicament, I certainly cannot assign any officers to such a case. However, I will issue a notice to all police, to be on the lookout for a..." he paused to read the description we gave him, "six-foot box with a picture on the side of a man climbing up a building. It should stand out, I would think."

Thanking him half-heartedly, we left the cop shop feeling very little relief. Austin jumped in the driver's seat and adjusted the rearview mirror slightly. "I assume we're going to continue combing the city."

"Uh-huh. We have no choice. We can't leave until we find the stupid thing."

"Otherwise, this whole trip was for nothing."

His statement caused me pause. "No Austin, you're wrong there. We've done some good on this journey. We reunited a family. Even if we don't get the Crazy box back, at least we've made a difference."

"Okay, Oprah," he replied with a chuckle.

"And I still have Tempest. And a hundred bucks."

"All right, now you're speaking my language!"

As the afternoon dragged on, we had combed an awful lot of the city, but had not found our prize. Unfortunately, in our searching, we had managed to work ourselves into a frenzy. Insanity might have been creeping in to our delicate psyches at this point. "I know what's going on here," Austin said after a long silence. "I've got it boiled down to two distinct possibilities. Both are keenly possible."

I held up my index finger. "Wait, let me guess. Is one of them a government conspiracy?"

"No, but that's good. I hadn't thought about government involvement. It would explain the cop. Okay, three possibilities. The others are aliens or the mob."

"Wait. By aliens, do you mean space creatures or guys from Mexico?"

My friend paused for a bit longer than would seem necessary, which meant he really had to think about it. That scared me. "No, it's gotta be space aliens. The Mexicans wouldn't have need for the cabinet."

"All right, sure. Maybe the space creatures have grown tired of abducting hicks and cows. But why would the mob want it?"

"Oh, you poor deluded fool!" He shouted this at me, and I knew I had to remove him from behind the wheel immediately. "The mob has always coveted arcade games. Why, back in the 60s..."

He tried to continue, but I interrupted his psychotic ranting. "Hey Austin, let's get some grub. Pull over at..." I realized we managed to drive back to Bob's Country Palace, and I sighed, "Bob's. I'm starting to miss the waitress."

"That could be the work of aliens too, ya know."

"I could believe that, sure." He slid into the only open spot in the lot and we hopped from the cab and trudged in. "She might even be an alien. I wonder what Planet Surly is like?"

"They probably have beer instead of water." As we sat, Austin continued to explain his bizarre hypotheses, going on for several minutes.

"Okay," I said, more to humor him than anything else, "I get the aliens. Sure, I buy the spaceship artwork possibility, and your unique 'probe gone wrong' explanation, but I still don't get the mob's connection in all this."

"No Jay, you're making it sound like they're in cahoots. That would be crazy. Why would the aliens need to work with the Mafia? No, the mob would have their own agenda here."

At that moment, Surly plodded over and when she saw us, shook her head slowly. "So what, you're just not gonna leave, are ya?"

"You'd miss us and you know it," I replied.

"Never a dull moment with y'all, that's fer sure." She thumbed toward Austin, still blathering on about the aliens, prompting her to ask, "What's fryin' his bacon?"

I rolled my eyes and sighed loudly. "Last night, someone stole the Crazy Climber cabinet from off our truck."

"The what?"

After spending a minute explaining, Austin added, "Yeah, we've wasted all day driving around looking for it. The cops weren't much help."

She snorted, so I'd assumed her experiences with the Nashville police mirrored our own. "Good luck with that."

"Thanks. So, uh, I guess two burgers and two beers."

"Ain'tcha boys getting' tired of burgers by now? It's all ya ever order here."

That comment snapped Austin out of his insane diatribe. "Whatdya mean? You told us that's all you serve!"

Chuckling, she said, "I was just messin' with ya. C'mon, really, what kinda restaurant only serves burgers?" She left and came back with menus, tossing them noisily on the table. "Oh my, you boys are so gullible." I had to use both hands to stop Austin from jumping up and throttling her on the spot.

When Surly came back with our meals, she asked, "So, where've y'all searched?" We did our best to draw her a verbal map. "Did you check Griffith Park, just south of here?"

"No. Why would we do that?"

"One thing I've noticed around here is that the homeless guys will take anything not nailed down. And a lot of 'em sleep in the park, once the shelter on Roselawn fills up, anyway. The city is pretty mindful of them being there, but they don't bother 'em too much."

Though I appreciated the advice for a new place to look, it didn't make sense to me. "Yeah, but why would a homeless guy steal an arcade cabinet?"

"Pretty colors? Firewood? A place to sleep? How would I know? But I've found if something's missing, check Griffith. And ya best hurry. It's gonna get dark soon."

Wolfing our dinners down as quickly as we could, we paid the bill and headed back to the truck. Opening the passenger side door, Austin began to giggle. "Can you imagine a bum sleeping in the Crazy Climber cabinet? He'd have to be all scrunched up."

"Or a real little guy. I dunno, but it might almost be worth the hassle to see something like that."

As the last of the daylight spilled out from the edge of the horizon, we found Griffith Park. I drove while Austin dug around in the glove box. "Hey, all right," he shouted when he found the large flashlight we had hoped would be in there. "Good old Phil, always planning ahead."

We turned the corner, and as the park came into view, we gasped at what we saw. There had to be twenty-five people sprawled haphazardly on the green grass. Some wore layers of thick, disheveled clothing, while others were wrapped in newspapers or tattered blankets. We also spotted a few with no extra covering at all, shivering in flimsy clothing in the cooling evening air.

When we caught sight of a patch of bright blue, we pulled over and stopped the truck. Jumping out and brandishing the flashlight, we walked over to get a closer look.

Yup, it was our bright blue tarp, wrapped around a man lying motionless on the ground. Only the soles of his worn shoes stuck out of the bottom, looking a bit like a giant blue burrito.

Austin began laughing out loud. "Oh my God, he's rolled like a massive Smurf joint!"

The two of us continued giggling at the sight, until my eyes fell upon the remnants of a fire next to the sleeping man. I began to say, "I can't believe the city would let them burn a fire in..." At that point, I noticed some bright colors protruding from the edge of the dying embers. Shining the flashlight at it, I saw a small bit of plastic with a picture of a skyscraper on it. Though bubbled up and charred, I could make out the gorilla standing on top of the building, as well as the orange and red colored letters C, R and A.

My eyes flew wide open as realization set in. I tossed the light all around the fire, and saw more bits of melted plastic as well as several pieces of blackened metal. Kicking at the fire, I dislodged the soot-covered coin box. "Oh no! Austin, they burned the cabinet! This guy burned my cabinet!"

Though normally a calm, peace-loving man, not overly prone to violent outbursts, when I fully comprehended what I saw, I lost it. After unleashing a deluge of swear words into the evening sky, I walked over to the bum. Still asleep and tightly wrapped in my tarp, I screamed at him while kicking him repeatedly on the souls of his worn sneakers. Not stirring in the least, I grabbed an edge of the tarp and yanked on it with all my might. "Get up, you bastard!" With Austin's assistance, we rolled the bum out of the tarp and onto the grass. He rolled a couple more feet before stopping. However, he must've been far too drunk or tired to take any notice of our actions. Although I could see him breathing, he remained asleep. This angered me all the more.

I handed Austin the flashlight as I approached the unconscious bum. When Austin lit him up, I gasped at what I saw. The guy looked terrible, with several layers of ripped and filthy clothes fluttering in the breeze. The few bits of exposed skin, like his cheeks and forehead, had blackened grime smeared across them. He smelled like a possum dipped in sewage, then dipped in whisky. Unfortunately for us, we stood downwind.

Seeing the man's shabby, disheveled appearance let a little bit of wind out of my sails, but I was still plenty volatile when a blinding light hit me in the face. "Hey, you two," came a powerful voice, "leave him alone! Step away, now!"

Turning, we saw a tall, stern man dressed in a sharp blue uniform and a shiny badge with the name Phillips printed on it.

Austin quickly replied, "This bum stole and destroyed our property, an arcade game cabinet."

I added loudly, "We drove all the way from Michigan to pick it up and this bastard ruined it!"

"First, I need you two to calm down." He pointed his long, narrow index finger at me. "I need you to drop the tarp and show me your ID. Then I'll need to see yours too," jabbing his finger at Austin.

Having a cop around forced me to calm down, but he clearly looked at us as the problems in this situation. Once Officer Phillips saw our drivers licenses, he said, "Michigan, huh? What are you doing in Nashville?"

"As I already said, we were driving an arcade game cabinet back home when this guy stole it and used it for firewood."

"An arcade game cabinet? Do you have any proof of ownership?"

"What?! Yes, I have the receipt and the police report I filed earlier today."

"Okay, I'll need to see that. Now, how can you prove who stole it?"

This question practically made me vibrate with anger. "That guy, right there, was sleeping in our tarp, the tarp that *was* covering the cabinet." As I pointed over at the bum, he finally started stirring. "Why don't ya ask him for yourself!"

"Again, I need you to calm down, sir. Why don't you two go get me the police report."

"Yes sir," Austin said meekly as he grabbed me by the arm and led me off toward the truck. Once we got there, he looked me in the eye. "Dude, I know you're pissed. We're both pissed here, but you've gotta calm down."

I exhaled a long, meaty sigh. "I know. Getting pissy with a cop won't help matters any. But dammit, we went through all of this and still don't have a cabinet!"

"I know, bud. But let's get the receipts, get this taken care of and get the hell outta this craptastic city."

When we returned with receipts in hand, we found Officer Phillips hunched on the ground, having a gentle conversation with the homeless guy. "I don't care how cold it was last night. We've had this talk before, Billy. You can't build fires in the park, and you can't take something just because you think it's trash. Everybody has rights."

"Me too, right?" He sounded like a child, and it sent shivers through me.

"Yes, Billy, you have rights too. Just remember, if it's cold outside, go to the shelter on Roselawn. Remember where Roselawn is, Billy?" When Billy shook his head rapidly, Phillips continued, pointing toward the road. "You just go to this street, walk that direction until you see the big gray building with all the windows. That's the shelter. Got it, Billy?"

Billy nodded again and this tough looking, crew-cut wearing cop smiled warmly and patted Billy on the shoulder. "Good. Why don't you go there now and get a meal."

As the homeless man staggered off down the road, he returned his attention to us. I handed the paperwork to him and he glanced at it for a moment. "Okay sirs, I am sorry about this situation. We do everything we can to keep the homeless off the street, but it's not an easy task." Walking over to the remnants of the fire, he kicked at it with a heavy black boot. "If this was your property, there is clearly little left. I'll take your information and add this to the report."

Once we finished speaking to Officer Phillips, there wasn't anything else to do, so we left Griffith Park.

## -TWENTY-TWO-

"Man," I sighed, "I don't know about you, but after that, I need a stiff drink."

Driving straight back to Bob's, we both got a double rum and Coke from Surly, our disgust and defeat evident upon our faces. "I don't even have to ask, do I?"

Austin shook his head slowly. "Oh, we found it, all right."

"It's a pile of ash and melted plastic."

"Sorry to hear it, boys."

Her momentary pleasantry made me look up at her. For the first time since we'd met her, she had a name tag on her blouse. "Is that really your name?"

She tossed me a queer expression. "Yeah. Why?"

"No way," Austin blurted out. "You're Surly Shirley?"

"I'm what!?" Oh, the glare she gave us could've melted plastic and blackened a metal coin box.

"Nothing," I said quickly. "It's a good name. It suits you."

And those were the last words Surly Shirley ever said to us. We gulped down our drinks, dropped a decent tip and skedaddled as fast as we could.

After the long day of driving and scouring the landscape, coupled with the depression of losing the cabinet, we knew we'd have to stay here one more lousy night. Not that we wanted to, of course, but we knew we wouldn't get far in our condition. "Man, do ya get the impression Nashville doesn't want us to leave?"

Paraphrasing an Eagles tune, I sang, "You can check out any time you like, but you can never leave Nashville."

As fate would have it, we booked the same room at the Vacation Inn for the third night in a row. This time, however, I didn't want to take any chances. Before we trudged up to our room, I made sure both Tempest and the monitor were completely covered with the now-stinky tarp, and I floated the night manager a twenty to keep an eye on the truck.

We had been in our beds for maybe an hour when someone began frantically knocking on our hotel room door. Austin, who sleeps like the dead, never heard it or even stirred in the slightest. When I heard the rapping, I feared it might be the night manager, coming to tell me all about how a group of little green men had just stolen Tempest. As I jumped out of bed, I heard a feminine voice yell, "Jay? Austin? Oh God, please be here!"

Marching quickly to the door, I peered out the peephole. "Kathy?"

I pulled the door open, and Kathy Spink dashed inside, pushing me aside to grab the door and force it shut. "Oh, thank God you two are still here! I wasn't sure I'd remembered the room number, or that you'd still be here, or..."

Dropping my hands upon her shoulders, I said sharply, "Calm down, Kathy. What are you still doing here? Shouldn't you be home by now?"

"Oh, I missed the last bus yesterday, and I wanted to say goodbye to a couple of people, but then..."

Out in the hall came a loud, bellowing voice. "Kathy! Where the hell are you? I know you're in one of these rooms! Get out here now, woman!"

I lowered my voice. "Who is that?"

"It's Mac! He's back!"

"Who?"

"Mac! My old boyfriend. The one who dragged me to Nashville! He spotted me at Bob's and now he wants me back. I told him no, that I was going back home, and he got so angry. I thought he was gonna hit me again, so I ran. I thought I lost him, but I guess he followed me. He..."

I shushed her as I heard pounding on the door across the hallway. Peering out the peephole, I watched the large, angry man interrogate the couple next door, before he turned and looked at my door. In a hushed tone, I said, "Go hide. I'll deal with this."

As I turned back to the door, he started pounding on it. Having no intention of letting the guy in, I continued to stare out the peephole until I heard him say, "I can see your eye, y'know. Is Kathy in there?"

Reluctantly, I opened the door. "Dude, what the hell?"

Shoving me aside, he forced himself into the room. I admonished myself mentally for not putting the chain lock on the door. This dude had me in every category. Standing several inches taller than me, his shoulders and arms rippled with tightly packed muscles. He had short, curly black hair and a tough, weatherworn face. This man clearly worked outdoors, with his hands, all his life. The sneer looked menacing enough, but his eyes really freaked me out. I could easily see the cold, harsh anger seething just beneath the surface. He scared me like I'd never been scared before. "She's in here, isn't she?"

Adrenaline coursing through my body had me wanting to flee, and I had to fight the urge to tell him the truth and run away like a coward. However, I held it together, reminding myself that he didn't know me from Adam, and had no proof of her whereabouts. Screwing up my courage, I screamed back, "Who the hell do you think you are, barging into my room like this? I oughta kick your ass, punk!"

At that point, Austin finally stirred awake. "Uh? Wha's goin' on?"

"Great," I yelled at Mac, "you woke my partner. I don't know who this Kathy chick is, but I've already called the cops. You need to leave. Now."

He stared down at me for an uncomfortably long time. Finally, he turned and left, muttering, "You're just lucky you're gay." I watched him through the peephole as he stomped away down the hall.

As quickly as I could, I slammed the door and locked it tight. I walked back into the room and collapsed on the bed. "Lord, I've never been so scared."

Austin, now fully awake, repeated his question. "What's going on? Who was that?" When Kathy crawled out from under Austin's bed, giving him quite the fright, he added, "And why was she under my bed?

Why are you even still here? And why did he call you gay?"

Still breathing heavily, I replied, "That's Mac. He's back to claim his lady, and we're not about to let that happen. Are we, partner?" I winked at him, which caused my heterosexual friend to cringe and roll away from us.

"The gay angle might've saved your life, y'know." Kathy allowed herself a fragile smile.

"Heh. Well, it wasn't intentional. And here I thought I stared him down like a manly man."

Kathy hugged me tightly and planted a kiss on my cheek. "You were very brave, Jay. My hero!"

"Not yet, I'm not. Do you know when the next bus rolls out?"

"There are several throughout the day, but I'd like to get on the one that leaves at nine."

"Okay, you'll be staying here tonight and in the morning, we'll get you on that bus. You can take my bed. I'll, um, I'll take the floor. Or maybe Austin will let me..."

A quick glance in his direction and I had to laugh. Fast asleep, he had already begun a snore cycle, starting off with a tiny, subtle snort. "Oh, we'd best get to sleep quickly. Austin's snore storm will build rapidly. So yeah, I'll grab that hunk of floor there."

Smiling devilishly, she replied, "No you won't. Um, how sound of a sleeper is he, anyway?"

"Very."

"Good to know."

The next morning, the three of us arose not long after sunrise. We gathered up our stuff and headed down to the pickup. "We'll get Ol' Red here packed up and we can head straight to the bus terminal. We might have time for breakfast, if we're quick enough."

Kathy wouldn't take her eyes off of me, which made me smile. "I enjoyed last night," she whispered in my ear.

Grinning, I nodded in her direction. "Me too. It was nice."

Austin hopped up in the truck bed and double-checked Tempest and the monitor's bungee cords. "What're you two talking about?"

"Nothing, Austy. We about ready?"

"Yup. Everything's tight and ready to..."

When I saw Austin's eyes widen, I knew to expect something awful. Kathy and I looked where Austin's gaze landed, and we saw why. Mac stood there in the parking lot, leaning up against his own pickup truck, a large, black beast shockingly reminiscent of the Wankermobile. "I knew you were lyin', boy." He walked over to Kathy and me, jamming a thick finger into her chest bone. "Baby, you're coming with me and there's not a damn thing the fruit here can do about it."

Part of me wanted to inform him of our activities last night – call me a fruit will ya – but I wisely refrained from such comments.

As he reached down to grab hold of her arm, Austin did something that shocked me. He took a running leap off the bed and slammed his body into Mac's left shoulder. The impact sent the scumbag sprawling to the ground, where he struck the side of his head against his tailgate. It must've stunned him, since he didn't immediately jump back up.

That gave us our chance. All three of us quickly dashed into Ol' Red, Austin at the wheel, Kathy in the middle and me on the right. He cranked the baby up, slammed it in reverse, and peeled out. Mac, who had just pulled himself to his feet, had to dive out of the way to avoid being squashed. Just like that, we hit the road and roared off with a squeal of our tires.

However, Mac had promptly come to his senses, and we had ourselves a street race! His black truck had some serious horsepower and he quickly approached us. Pulling up along the passenger side, he swerved and slammed into us, impacting just behind the door. Though he didn't ram us very hard, it pushed us out of our lane, causing a couple of horns to blare around us. Austin muscled Ol' Red back into our lane.

As he rolled up to ram us a second time, Austin yelled, "Oh my God, more lunatics in pickups! Why does this keep happening?"

"Worse yet, we have morning traffic to contend with this time!"

"This happen to you guys a lot?" Kathy asked.

"Oh sure, yeah. Didn't ya see all the dents?"

The maniac rammed into us again, pushing Ol' Red sharply to the left and directly into oncoming traffic. Deftly maneuvering, Austin shot even further into opposing traffic, flying around the startled drivers in a wide arc. Spotting a side street, he wrenched on the brakes and spun the wheel frantically, shooting past several more cars, their horns blaring and tires screeching in cacophonous unity.

Though it didn't buy us much time before Mac found a neighboring side street and caught up to us, it gave me a few precious moments to think and remember.

Elbowing Kathy, I pointed at the driver's seat. "Reach down between Austin's legs, quickly!"

In near unison, they both replied, "Excuse me?"

"Under his seat. Grab the bat!"

Doing as I ordered, she procured my old aluminum baseball bat, handing it to me as Mac roared up next to us again. As I rolled down the window, I looked back at Kathy. "Grab hold of me!" She gripped the back of my belt as I leaned out the window. "Hold me tight!"

As he approached, I raised the bat and swung, breaking off his side mirror. He tried to pull away from us, but Austin mirrored his movement. I whacked twice more, whiffing the first time but hitting his front windshield squarely with the second, shattering a decent-sized section in his vision area. "Yeah, take that!"

Clearly not taking it well, he swerved sharply into us. I tried to pull myself inside as quickly as possible and I barely made it, but the jarring motion caused my grip on the bat to loosen. It fell, clattering upon the pavement. "Crap!"

The last hit pushed us off the road, and gravel spit out from our tires as we began to fishtail. Austin did an amazing job of steering and kept us from flying out of control. We went up a grassy embankment a bit faster than any of us would've liked and we were momentarily airborne. Feeling a horrific flashback, I spun my head around and watched the Tempest machine intently.

Fortunately, Austy had done a masterful job of bungeeing it and the monitor, and everything held firm. I breathed a sigh of relief as we hit pavement with our payload intact.

"There!" Kathy pointed toward a major intersection. "Turn right! We're almost at the terminal!"

The light at this intersection had been red since we spotted it. Knowing it would be a tricky proposition, making a sharp turn onto a major intersection with the light against us, Austin instead opted for a radically different approach. "Hold tight!" He yelled as he slammed on the brakes at the last possible moment. We skidded and screeched to a stop, our front tires nipping at the crosswalk.

Though he had his brakes floored as well, Mac screamed past us and into oncoming traffic, where a fifty-three foot semi-truck solidly greeted him. We watched in horror as the semi T-boned his black pickup truck, his window glass exploding like a detonated bomb. His truck flipped side over side repeatedly, eventually coming to rest on the passenger side door after several revolutions.

Though relief flowed through us, none of us wanted to see the bad man killed. So, we sat there, waiting for the light to change, looking for any sign of movement. After about a minute, he pushed his mangled door open and flopped to the pavement. We all exhaled our sighs of relief.

When the light turned to green, Austin casually turned right and drove us to the bus station in a calm and peaceful manner.

"Oh my God, I can't thank you two enough." Kathy gave Austin a solid bear hug and a peck on the cheek. You risked your lives for me." Then she walked up to me, her smile beaming. "And you, you went above and beyond to help out a total stranger, a common thief no less. I stole from you and you did all this to help me. I still don't get why you did it."

I shrugged. "Honestly, I don't know either. I guess you looked like you needed help, and I guess I was right, huh?"

She nodded as a tear formed in the corner of her left eye. "I'm going to miss you, Jay." With that, she pulled me in and gave me the mother of all kisses.

"I'll miss you too, Kathy."

"Whoa," Austin breathed, "what did I miss last night?"

Austin and I stood at the boarding gate, watching until she climbed aboard her bus. We didn't leave until it pulled away. "We done a good thing, Austy my friend."

"Uh-huh. But seriously Jay, what did I miss last night? Where exactly did she sleep?"

My grin had to say it all, but I spoke anyway. "I'm not one to kiss and tell. But you can call me Flashdrive II."

"Uh, no I can't. Seriously, I can't."

Oh, we'd had quite enough of Nashville, so we immediately hit the highway and drove for about an hour before stopping for food. Spotting a nice, quiet Burger Jack just off the highway, we went inside to grab a quick meal before hitting the road for home.

Gnawing on a Big Jack, I lifted the bun and plucked the two pickles out, tossing them onto the tray with a barely audible splat. "Well, my friend, things didn't end up as I had planned."

Austin slurped on a Coke as he replied. "No, definitely not. I'm sorry, man."

"Yeah, me too." Although I thought about it for a moment, then added, "However, it certainly wasn't all bad. Y'know, reuniting a family was kinda cool. I won a video game contest. That was pretty sweet."

"We both got laid! A definite highlight."

"Yes, that is true. Good memories there."

Swallowing his bite of Quarter Pound Jack, he continued, "We did meet a lot of wonderful people."

"And those who weren't wonderful felt our wrath."

"Our wrath, Jay?"

"Well, ya know what I mean. Mac won't soon forget us."

"True dat."

"And it's not like I'm coming home empty handed. I do have a Tempest machine and a monitor, after all.

So I can still fix Crazy. I'll need to buy yet another cabinet, of course."

Austin pointed his index finger, waggling it at me sternly. "Dude, before you ask, I am *not* coming with you on any more road trips."

That caused a laugh to escape me. "Don't worry about that. I have no intention of driving for any more cabinets."

As we pushed the fast food restaurant's door open to feel a rush of warm, late-morning air, Austin asked, "Are we really going home now?"

Grinning broadly, I replied, "We sure are, little buddy!"

"Man, my yard's gotta look like a forest by now."

"Austin, your yard always looks like a forest."

"It won't in the winter," he corrected me.

"Technically, it'll look like a snow-covered forest then."

"Dude, just get in the truck."

"I'll bet you'll have bears and pumas hunting for deer in your yard. Yeah, they'll use the tree-like weeds for cover."

"Shut up already!"

"Oh, I know! You should film a documentary. Nature in the City, a cautionary tale of the pitfalls of not keeping your lawn mowed."

"Get. In. The. Truck."

"Okay, okay."

- TWENTY-THREE -

We definitely felt the strong desire to get ourselves home, and we tried awfully hard to drive straight there. However, we knew we had no choice but to stop a couple of times for gas and food.

At the last stop, in a mid-sized town near the Ohio border, we pulled into a place called The Waffle Hut. Our funds dwindling, we wanted to feed our faces and bolt as soon as we could.

After placing our orders, the waitress, a young, perky blonde with incredibly white teeth asked us, "So, where ya headed?"

"Back home to Michigan, my dear," Austin said proudly. "Can't wait! My bed's beckoning me to get home!"

"Mine's a waterbed, so it's gurgling in yearning."

"That's funny," she replied with a much-obliged fake giggle. "Where ya been?"

With that simple question, we bored her for the next several minutes. Once we completed our tale, I tossed my thumb out the big, picture window next to our booth. "See the tarp? Tempest is under that."

"Y'know, if you guys like video games, there's an arcade down on Miller. I haven't been in that part of town in a while, but I'd be surprised if it wasn't still there. You should go check it out."

I casually thanked her and instantly dismissed the notion. Frankly, I had more of an urge to get back on the road than I did to play any more video games.

Glancing over at Austin, the life in his eyes astonished me. "I'm up for playing a couple of games. Bet they have Galaga!"

Apparently, we had one more stop. "Betcha a quarter they don't."

"You're on!"

Once we completed choking down our less-than-gourmet Waffle Hut meals and begged directions from the waitress, we hopped in the truck and rolled over to Miller Avenue.

It took several minutes of traversing the street to find the place. Though several machines still sat inside the building, they had gone out of business quite some time ago. The windows were caked with grime and the machines wore a layer of dust. I turned to Austin and said, "Well, the waitress would be surprised."

"What?"

"She said she'd be surprised if...oh, never mind. But hey," I added, digging into my pocket, "you technically won the bet." Just on the other side of the dirty front picture window stood a Galaga machine. I flicked him an old quarter.

As we turned to hop back in the truck, we found ourselves facing several teenage boys. All but one sat straddling their bikes, the bikeless one standing on a flame-covered skateboard. They all seemed decent enough, meaning none of them looked too thuggish, so I greeted them warmly. "Hello, boys. Hey, how long's this place been closed?"

The largest one of the group, a thick behemoth with only the thinnest of fuzz protruding from his shaven head replied, "Closed last winter. We used to hang out here."

"Still do, actually," added a smaller kid with a tiny, wispy bit of fur on his upper lip, something he probably referred to as a mustache. Oh, to be young again! "No place else to go."

The small kid on the skateboard pointed up at the tarp on our truck. "What's that?"

Austin hopped up and quickly yanked the tarp off. "Tempest! Fantastic game. Did they have one in there?"

"Oh yes," the behemoth replied with a toothy grin, "I used to crush that game."

"You sucked, Brad. I was better!"

"In your dreams, moron."

I grinned at their camaraderie. "Ya boys wanna play? All ya need is a quarter and a place for us to plug in."

They all whooped it up, so we ended up plugging in at the gas station next door, with their blessing. The owners of the station, a cranky old couple, were happy not to have the hoodlums, as they referred to them, spending all day behind the vacant arcade breaking bottles, smoking cigarettes and laughing too hard. Although they probably spent the next couple hours laughing just as hard, they did not destroy anything. And we made a few bucks. Not that we needed the money, really, but it felt a bit like old time's sake.

While the skateboard kid played, Austin and I sat on the curb talking to the others. Austin, trying to suppress a grin, asked the boys their opinions about Y2K. "You guys think the world's gonna end?"

"Naw, man," said the big kid. "Ain't no big deal."

As the others laughed boisterously, one kid shook his head slowly. About my height, he had a thick, messy mane of curly brown hair and a bit of an acne problem. "I've read up on it. They're working on it as we speak, so it'll probably be fine, but it could get real bad."

"Bad?" The big kid slapped his friend sharply on the back. "It's just computers, Dave. What's the big deal?"

"Dude." Dave's eyes grew large. "Don't ya get it? Computers run everything. Everything! The banks could lose everyone's money, the gas pumps could stop working, even the government computers might crash."

"So, why should we care? We don't drive or have bank accounts or care about the government."

"The government controls all sorts of stuff," I interjected, "like the missiles, the nuclear power plants, the water, even the electricity. Worst case scenario has all the nuclear power plants overheating and melting down, water and sewage separation failing, mass power outages, even warheads firing on their own."

"End of the world," Austin said with an evil grin. "Even your home computers and video game systems might crash."

"Whoa," the wispy-mustached one breathed. "Never heard it put that way. Dude, that sucks."

"Man," the big kid added. "I'm too young…"

When all the kids stopped laughing and began to look downright morose, I felt the need to interject. "Ah, we're just messin' with ya."

"Yeah," Austin added, "that's worst-case stuff there. It could even be comical. Maybe the ball won't drop on New Year's, or it'll drop too fast. Wouldn't that rock? It'll probably be fine. Probably."

Our comments didn't snap them out of their funk, so I thought I'd lighten the mood. "Y'know boys, you're looking at the arcade master of Bradenton, Florida. Who here thinks they can beat me in a game of Tempest?"

After the big kid soundly thrashed me at my own game, the teens began to enjoy themselves again.

Once they had all played a few games each, some of their friends came over and gave it a try as well.

At that point, we started thinking about packing it in when a late-model Chrysler whipped rapidly into the parking lot. A tall, pale man jumped out and glared at us. He had a thin, well-maintained beard and a triangle of reddish-brown chest hair protruding from the top of his button-down shirt. Striding up to us, he jabbed his finger and yelled, "Hey, what's the big idea here?"

Puzzled, Austin replied, "Whatdya mean?"

"I mean, you broke into my arcade and stole my Tempest, didn't you? I have a good mind to call the cops!"

I tossed my hands in the air. "Whoa now, wait a second, buddy. This is our machine. We bought it in Florida. I have the receipt."

Austin folded his arms, presumably in an attempt to look menacing. "Yeah, check your building, dude. It's still secure."

"It better be," the redheaded man replied with no lapse in his hostility.

I left him to chat with Austin while I grabbed the receipt. Upon showing it to him, he calmed considerably. "Geez guys, I'm sorry about that. I just saw you two there with the game, and I got pissed. There have been some break-ins in the past few months."

"It's all right, pal. Oh, I'm Jay and that's Austin." I offered my hand in friendship.

He took my hand in a mushy, clammy embrace. "Hi fellas. I'm Gary."

Austin pointed at the disheveled building. "So, you have a locked building full of video games. Couldn't make a living in the arcade business, huh?"

"Nah. It belonged to my father. He willed it to me a couple years ago. I never really cared much for games, but I tried to make it work. No one's playing games anymore."

Pointing over at the kids on our truck, I said, "Well, I don't know about that, Gary. We've seen probably a dozen kids, and made probably five bucks off of one game."

"Eh, five bucks won't pay the electricity."

"Sure," Austin added, "I get it. But why just abandon them? Why not sell 'em off? At least you'd make something."

"What, ya don't think I've tried? I put ads in the paper, but I only sold a couple."

"Haven't you tried eBay yet?" I asked.

Gary looked clearly puzzled. "E what?"

"eBay. It's an online auction house. People use it to buy and sell across the world."

"Really?" When Gary's eyes lit up, we knew we could help one more person on our journey.

"Sure thing. That's how I found out about..." I started to point at the truck, but realization hit me. "Well, not Tempest. I had a Crazy Climber cabinet, but it was destroyed."

"Destroyed?"

"Yeah," I sighed. "A homeless guy stole it right off this truck and actually used it as firewood."

"Ew. I can't even imagine what the smoke smelled like." He paused before continuing. "So, um, do you know what some of these machines might be worth?"

"Well, somewhat, I guess."

A huge grin widened upon Gary's hairy face. "Would you care to come inside? Maybe you'll see something you like."

Austin and I exchanged glances. Neither of us wanted to bother, but the kids still stood three-deep in line to play Tempest, so we shrugged and followed him up to the door. Gary produced a key chain and after a few attempts, he found the right key to unlock the door to his family's old arcade.

Though covered with dust, the games looked to be in decent shape. Neither of us really had a clue, so we walked around with him, pointed at various machines and made up numbers. "Oh, the Galaga, that would probably net you five or six hundred, easily. It's still very popular. We paid four hundred for our Tempest, and oh, that Gravitar is kinda rare, it might get ya..." I paused when I saw, in the far corner away from the others, a familiar machine. "Hey, you got Crazy Climber!"

"Oh, yeah. It died a while back."

My eyes lit up. "Really? Can we see it?" Austin and I dashed over to it and wiped off the dust. The cabinet looked very nice, and when I opened it up, it had all the components. "How did it die?"

Gary shrugged. "I have no idea. Remember, I know nothing about these things."

I pulled my wallet from my back pocket and opened it. "Can I buy it? I only have a hundred and seventeen bucks left."

"For a dead game? Sure, that's fine."

Beaming, I handed him all my remaining cash.

Not too long after I made the transaction, the kids finished playing, so we packed everything up and got back on the road to Michigan.

"Man, that rocked," Austin said with a chuckle.

"Yeah, it sure did. Not only did we get yet another cabinet, but we made a bit over seven dollars off of Tempest to boot."

We sat silent for a second before I added, "Y'know Austin, I'm really gonna miss that."

"Me too, bud. Good times."

Though we hit a traffic jam upon entering our home state, due to construction, of course, we made fairly decent time. Before the last rays of a magnificent, fiery sunset had faded beyond the horizon, we found ourselves sleeping in our own beds.

# - TWENTY-FOUR -

Monday morning felt strange to me. After three weeks off, being back at my desk didn't feel right. I sat there in my cubicle for a while, trying to figure out what I needed to be doing. Fortunately, my boss came over and tapped me on the shoulder. "Jay, please follow me into Mr. Quinten's office."

"Oh. Okay, sure." I swallowed hard when I realized I had only seen the inside of Mr. Quinten's office twice, once when they hired me, and the other time when I hit Octavio Banyon in the face with a box of jumbo paper clips. Long story.

"Hello, Mr. Quinten," I said nervously. Trying to make small talk, I added, "I like what you've done with the place. The ficus needs some water, I think."

Looking at me funny, he said sharply, "The plant is plastic, Jay. Anyway, the reason I called you in here has to do with your three week absence."

Oh wow. Funny, I should've seen this coming, and thus prepared more. I totally blanked out on my excuse. Crap! Seemed like it had something to do with pork. Pork? What the heck? "Oh yeah, sorry. But I'm back now, ready and raring to work."

"I see that, Jay. But we need to discuss a few things."

"Sure thing, boss. Like what?"

He flipped open a manila folder with *Naylor, Jaymond* stenciled on the flap. "You apparently called in due to a death in the family, your grandmother. But later, it turned out she didn't die, but then your grandfather became ill." Pausing, he looked up at me and squinted slightly. "What was this illness, exactly?"

"What does it say there?"

"I want to hear it from you."

"Uh…" Then it hit me, and I wanted to rest my head on his desk. "A contagious pork gout coma, if I remember correctly. I, uh, I thought I had it briefly too, but it turned out to be gas… really bad gas."

Mr. Quinten shook his head very slowly. "Yes, the two are commonly confused. Mr. Naylor, I don't actually have to say the words *you're fired*, do I?"

"If you wouldn't mind, sir."

Since I already felt like crap, I figured I'd better take care of another dreaded task. I went home, switched my Saturn for Ol' Red, and drove Phil's battered truck back to his house. "You're a couple weeks late, y'know" he said with a controlled amount of displeasure. "You're just lucky I kept on stopping by your house to feed your cat. That cat of yours is nuts, by the way. Did you see the damage she caused?"

"Uh, yeah, yeah I did. Say, speaking of damage..." I figured I may as well use the segue he served me. "Ya might wanna come out and take a gander at Ol' Red."

Under different circumstances, I might've found a morbid bit of pleasure watching Phil's range of emotions. His demeanor changed from annoyance, to mild joy at seeing me, to shock when he saw the state of his beloved truck, and rapidly finding its way to seething anger. He let loose with a few choice expletives before saying, "What did you do to my truck?!"

"Oh, that's a series of amusing stories," I told him. "But hey, I'm sure you're busy right now. So here's your key. Call me after you calm down and I'll fill ya in. She's a real trooper, by the way. Gave us no trouble at all." I took one step off the porch before realization set in. "Oh, um, I'm gonna need a ride home."

It turned out to be a good day to walk four miles.

Back at home, I spent a bit of time working on Crazy. At first, I plugged the dead machine in, just to confirm its lack of life. True to form, it didn't light up. So I started swapping out pieces, one at a time, until I found the offending part. Once it powered up, I danced around like a fool for a minute, then played a couple games.

So, though I had no job, I did have two arcade games. Tempest played like a dream, with a tight spinner and a sharp monitor free of burn-in. And now, so did Crazy.

I sat on a chair in the garage, staring at my two games, thinking of what all I went through to get them. Man, did I have fun, driving from town to town, meeting people and watching them playing my games. My, what a neat, unique adventure we had.

Then, a thought struck me.

- TWENTY-FIVE -

Several days later, just after noon, I found myself on the phone, listening to ring after ring.

Finally, after many dozens of rings, I heard the voice. "Uhhh. Hullo?"

"Hey Austin, it's Jay. What're ya doing for the rest of the summer?"

"Huh?"

"Once you've managed to wake up, come over. I got something you'll find... interesting."

"Oh, goody." The sarcasm oozed from his words.

It took him a couple of hours, but when he showed up, he looked understandably puzzled. "Uh, what's that?"

235

"That," I replied, "is a food services vehicle." It opened from the side with steps that pulled down and an upper half that lifted up.

"So, um, you're going into the food services industry? Like one of those traveling food carts ya see at carnivals?"

"Not quite. It's slightly modified." With that simple fanfare, I lifted the top to reveal a nicely carpeted inside area, complete with three arcade games lined up in a row. In addition to Crazy and Tempest, I had a Galaga. "I had to get Galaga."

"Cool. So, uh, what's this all about?"

I smiled broadly as I made the announcement. "It's my, or I should say *our* new business, if you're interested. We're going to be a traveling arcade. I got the other machine cheap, the truck is used, and I got Phil to help with the labor to turn it into an arcade vehicle."

"I can't believe he's still speaking to you after what happened to Ol' Red."

"Well, after I explained to him how my insurance would cover the damage from hitting that herd of deer," I paused to wink, "he calmed down considerably."

"Lovely. What's a little insurance fraud among friends?"

"Exactly. But anyway, look at this! It has a generator built in to the corner, so we won't need to siphon off power or rely on the kindness of strangers to run the machines. We just drive around, find a parking lot or a state park, get permission where applicable, and collect the cash."

"I must say I'm marginally impressed." This came from a female voice behind us. We spun around to bear witness to my old girlfriend Bonnie. I hated to admit it, but her presence made my heart momentarily skip a beat. She wore a tight-fitting pink tank top and a short cotton skirt. Her long, blonde hair had been spiraled up into a tight bun, skewered at a forty-five degree angle by a blue Bic pen. "I doubt you'll make enough money to survive, mind you, but at least you're thinking about your future, somewhat."

Even though the old attraction flooded through me like a faucet cranked all the way open, I did my best to subdue it. "What are you doing here, Bonnie?"

"I'm just here to get my stuff. You sure were gone a while."

"Yeah, long story. Go on in and grab whatever you want. I'll be in momentarily."

Once she entered the house and shut the door, I turned to Austin and reinitiated my beaming smile. "So anyway, whatdya think? Pretty cool, huh?"

"It is, Jay. Say, I'll take a look around here. You need to go deal with the princess."

Sighing, I replied, "I know. All right." With that, I trudged into my house.

She already had a Hefty bag partially filled with her clothes, and had moved into the bathroom. I popped my head around the corner as she dropped the hair dryer into a box. "Oh, uh, that's mine."

"No, I bought this when yours burned out."

"Really? When did that happen?"

"Over two months ago, Jay. Do ya see what I'm talking about? You never pay any attention to your surroundings."

I found myself smiling, which threw her off guard. "Yup, it's true. I know I've been sleep walking through my life for far too long. This trip opened my eyes. I experienced things I never could've imagined a few months ago. Met some people, lived through adversity, even helped reunite a family."

After I spent a few minutes recanting our adventure, perhaps embellishing how I single-handedly won a bar fight, but accurately describing how I reunited Kathy and her parents, she had a slightly different look in her eyes. She turned away, grabbing up her toothbrush and shampoo, but our eyes caught and locked in the mirror. She turned back, set the items in her bag, and gently laid her hands on my shoulders. We embraced, and that embrace turned into a lingering kiss. When she pulled back, she said softly, "Hard to believe a couple of weeks could change you so much. The bar fight seems especially hard to believe."

"I know, I could hardly believe it myself. But yeah, I've changed. I've grown as a person."

She looked deeply into my eyes, and placed a hand on my cheek. "I'm glad for you, really. But it doesn't change anything between us."

"Oh good Lord, of course it doesn't!" I said with a bit more intensity than I had intended. "What I mean is, during this trip, I came to realize something. You're right. We're definitely not made for each other. I need someone more laid back, while you need a more structured and disciplined man. I will always cherish the time we've had together Bonnie, but this trip taught me a thing or two about what I want. And it's not you."

For a fleeting moment, I saw the hurt in her eyes, before a wave of anger flooded into them. At first, I wondered where the animosity came from, but then it occurred to me. Even though she agreed with everything I said, I suspect she wanted this breakup to be her idea.

Having nothing else to say, I spun on my heels and strolled out into the yard.

As I approached Austin, who was sitting on the carpeted steps of the new Crazymobile, he stood up and asked, "So, how'd it go in there?"

Grinning, I replied, "Brutally fantastic! Or fantastically brutal, depending on your point of view. She's grabbing her stuff now. In fact, looks like she's about done."

Kicking the screen door open, she stormed out with both arms full of bags. As she passed us, she yelled sarcastically, "Oh, don't worry, I don't need any help."

Austin surprised me by dashing over and popping open her car door, sporting a huge grin. Bonnie, clearly taken aback, looked at him with a puzzled expression. "Uh, thanks, Austin."

"Hey, I'm just helping to facilitate you getting the hell outta here as quickly as possible." When she narrowed her eyes at him, he added, "Y'know, I always hated that passive-aggressive crap you spewed whenever you saw me. I've been a good friend to Jay, and I could've been a good friend to you as well, but you never gave me the chance. But it's too late now, sister. Hit the bricks."

Bonnie started to say something, but instead she groaned loudly, hopped in her Toyota and sped off.

"You have no idea how long I've wanted to say that to her," Austin said with a wide, wicked grin.

"Well, at least a year, I take it."

"Oh, I hated her even before I knew she existed. The space-time continuum rippled with her evil."

I started to contest his use of the word *evil*, but I saw no point, so I let it slide. "Well, that's that. So anyway, whatdya think of this thing, huh?"

Austin walked back to the steps, turned and looked in for a moment. When he turned back, his expression had changed. "It's great, Jay. But really, I just don't see how we can make a living with this. Three video games, a generator and a gas guzzling truck?"

I quickly interjected. "It gets nearly the same mileage as Ol' Red. We can charge fifty cents per game. Double our profits."

"Where we gonna sleep?"

"Oh, we can pick up a nice tent for campgrounds, or if we do well, we can splurge on a hotel room. There is room in the back for us to sleep on the floor, if it comes to that."

With a heavy, lengthy sigh, Austin looked me square in the eyes. "Sorry man, but I can't do it. This has been a blast, but I'll be thirty-two in a few months. I'm getting too old for this kid stuff. I have responsibilities." When I looked at him funny, he reworded it. "What I mean is, I have a house, I have rent anyway, a car payment, all my stuff. What would I do with all my stuff? You gotta think about the same thing. I'm renting, but this house is yours. You have a mortgage." He saw the hangdog look in my eyes, which caused him to get a bit sadder himself. "I don't mean to rain on your parade, but we both need to grow up and think about our futures. If I were smart, I would go back to school, finish up my degree and try to get a real job with a good company. This arcade thing is something ya do when you're eighteen, fresh outta school, with your whole life ahead of you. This would be like the rich kids' equivalent of back-packing across Europe." He set his hand on my shoulder and patted it. "Sorry man. I need to get going. I'll talk to ya tomorrow, okay?"

I watched him hop in his car and drive away. He never looked back at me, and I never took my eyes off of him.

After I went inside and plopped down on the couch, I looked around my cluttered house. Even though I knew he spoke the truth, I felt so betrayed. He wasn't supposed to be the one who thought about such blasé things as the future and being an adult. That was the last thing I expected from Austin Ridenour. What happened to the 'I just quit my job to drive to Weedpatch with you' guy? I never saw this coming.

I couldn't bear to think about it anymore. Exhaustion crept hard into my soul, so I slumped over and passed out on the couch, using a pile of my dirty clothes as a makeshift pillow.

- TWENTY-SIX -

After battling a demon made of dirty clothes in my dreams, I jarred myself awake. Apparently, I had to bite the beast to force it to release its grip on me, since I had the tip of a tube sock dangling from the corner of my mouth. Spitting it out, I stumbled over to the bathroom, to quickly gargle with some mouthwash.

Afterwards, I ambled into the kitchen and managed to find a couple food items not completely spoiled. The can of minestrone soup and a frost-covered ham and cheese Hot Pocket greeted my taste buds with complete disregard for my safety. But as I gnawed away at the Hot Pocket, after dipping it in the soup to try to soften it up, I allowed my mind to run through what Austin had said to me.

The bottom line, I realized, was I had already bought and modified the truck. Regardless of anything else, I owned it, so I may as well utilize it. Now, while he spoke the truth about having a life here, what with a house, car and all the trappings therein, I still had a rather unique opportunity parked in my driveway.

At that moment, I came to a realization. I didn't need to be global here, or even full time, for that matter. Easily enough, I could hit some Michigan fairs and festivals, perhaps even find a campground and set up shop. I could get a weekday job and do that on the weekends.

Somewhere around this messy house of mine, I stashed the State Journal's yearly listing of all the fairs and festivals in the greater Lansing area. After spending a few minutes digging through piles of unread magazines and catalogs, I located it. Using that list, I started making phone calls.

It took several calls, and I had to deal with a fair amount of rejection. It was a bit late, in many cases, to try to book myself into these events. But when the head of the DeWitt Ox Roast granted me permission to park my arcade wagon on Bridge Street, I jumped up, started dancing around the house, yelling "Woohoo" at the top of my lungs, and once again, freaking out my poor cat.

Regardless of what Austin said last night, and despite the fact that he wouldn't be awake at this early hour, I snatched the phone as I boogied past it and dialed his number. It rang only four times before I heard a pounding on my door.

With the phone still in hand, I walked over to the door and swung it open. A grinning, sleep depraved Austin stood there. I held my cordless phone in the air. "Man, go home and answer your phone already."

He shuffled in and plopped down on my couch. "Hey, I got to thinking about what I said. It occurred to me that we don't need to do this thing full time."

I couldn't help but laugh. Great minds, or perhaps warped minds, do think alike. "Dude, you ruined my punch line. When you answered the phone, all groggy n' stuff, I was gonna say, 'What are ya doing Saturday, August twenty-first?' You were gonna say, 'What?' and I'd tell ya. So say 'what,' already."

"Huh?"

I shrugged. "Close enough. I got us a gig at the Ox Roast!"

The DeWitt Ox Roast, being our hometown festival and all, was a major coup for us. Austin, not usually one for demonstrating emotion, jumped around just like I did.

On that hot, muggy Saturday in August, things couldn't have gone better. Austin and I debuted *Driving Crazy*, a fitting name for our traveling arcade business, I felt. The money we made, while not great, was a lot better than either of us had expected. Thinking ahead, we had flyers and business cards printed up, handing them out in droves. Due to our marketing blitz, and a few more phone calls, we secured a couple more assignments at other season-ending festivals, including Grand Ledge's Color Cruise and Island Festival in October. They let us set up right on the island.

That kicked open the door for us. By the start of the year 2000 festival season, we managed to book at least one weekend a month, with three in a row in June. From there, we started slowly branching out, going up into northern Michigan and down into northern Ohio.

By the next season, we had snagged shows in the Upper Peninsula as well as the rest of Ohio. Then we stretched into Illinois, Indiana and Wisconsin. After that, Driving Crazy expanded to a bigger vehicle with more games. We started having some gigs on weekdays, as well. After that, we needed a second vehicle.

It didn't take long before we quit our regular jobs, and became a full time traveling arcade.

Y2K had come and gone, with lots of hoopla, fear and panic. But little came of the world-ending, computer-crashing, civilization-crumbling nonsense many had prophesized. It did, however, change the lives of two silly blokes who never wanted to grow up. Fortunately for us, it turned out we didn't have to.

# DRIVING CRAZY